"Lily . . . I want to see you again.

She let a moment go by. "And you like being able to get what you want," she returned, a glint of emerald in her eyes. "Don't you, Dylan?"

He recognized that she was quoting his own words back at him. "Yes," he replied with devastating simplicity. "I do." His mobile, sensually shaped lips twisted. "Lily, I can't *order* you to see me again—"

"But you can ask." There was the faintest hint of flirtation in her voice, the first Dylan had heard that evening.

"Oh, I will ask," he promised. Lifting his hand, he gently traced the graceful curve of her cheek. Her skin was very smooth against his fingers. Several silken strands of her hair had worked loose and were blowing across her face. He tucked them back behind her ear in a gesture that held more than a trace of possessive intimacy. "The evening wasn't supposed to end like this," he told her, the look in his amber-brown eyes as frank as his tone of voice.

Lily trembled for an instant, then went still. Her pulse had started racing as soon as he'd begun caressing her face. "Dylan—" she whispered. "Dyl—"

Carole Buck

Born on the Fourth of July, Carole Buck was raised in Connecticut and now makes her home in Atlanta. Although she had ambitions to be a ballerina, a lawyer, an archaeologist, and a spy, she somehow ended up as a television news writer and entertainment reporter. She spends a lot of time in the dark, because she is also a movie reviewer. Her greatest fantasy is to travel back in time.

Carole is single. She says her men friends are always offering to help her do research for her romance novels. Her woman friends want introductions to the heroes she writes about. Carole just wishes her characters would remember she's supposed to be in charge.

Life, says Carole, is a banquet, and she intends to fill her plate to the fullest as many times as she can.

Other Second Chance at Love books by
Carole Buck

ENCORE #219
INTRUDER'S KISS #246
AT LONG LAST LOVE #261
LOVE PLAY #269
FALLEN ANGEL #289
MR. OCTOBER #317
SWANN'S SONG #334

Dear Reader:

It takes a darn fine writer to capture the emotional acrobatics of two creatively frustrated, romantically cautious, and generally mischievous housemates as vividly—and endearingly—as Laine Allen does in *Tangling With Webb* (#346). Historical romance writer Cristy McKnight is tired of quivering virgins and dastardly villains; spy thriller author Webb Cannon has had it with slick undercover operatives and faithless female double agents. In a quirky about-face, Cristy and Webb reverse writing roles ... and soon both they *and* their fictional creations are caught in the stickily complicated—and suddenly sensual—web of this uproarious tale.

Next, I'm thrilled to introduce our latest SECOND CHANCE AT LOVE "discovery," new author Kerry Price, whose light, sparkling *Frenchman's Kiss* (#347) presents Jean-Claude Delacroix, a hero no woman could resist. Spunky Sherry Seaton is knocked off-balance when the sexy, charming, thoroughly enticing Frenchman sweeps her into a world of sophisticated glamour and whimsical fun. It all begins with what Sherry mistakenly assumes is an obscene phone call. Further complications arise when she meets Jean-Claude at a hotel room during a blackout—and he takes full advantage of the situation's sensual possibilities! Jean-Claude's methods may be madness, but he's irresistible—and so is *Frenchman's Kiss*.

In *Kid at Heart* (#348), Aimée Duvall returns with all the zest and zaniness you've come to expect. Here, wacky toy designer Lisa Fleming and company owner Chase Sanger team up to invent a new line of playthings ... and discover they'd rather fool around with each other. Who'd think a sophisticated, urbane guy like Chase could become such an uninhibited, fun-loving playmate? But Lisa seems to attract confusion, and Chase has a hard time maintaining his businesslike demeanor when confronted with a robot gone berserk or a group of appallingly inventive six-year-olds—not to mention his own eccentric family. In *Kid at Heart*, love, and Aimée Duvall, make anything possible!

Helen Carter's latest romance is my personal favorite. She's always been a pro at creating complex, deeply sympathetic characters, but in *My Wild Irish Rogue* (#349) she surpasses her previous accomplishments with a prim and proper sociologist heroine and a carefree, pleasure-seeking (but never irresponsible!) hero. In Liam Clare, Helen combines Irish charm and American ingenuity, masculine strength and penetrating insight, to form a perfect hero—one who challenges Ingrid to open herself to new possibilities, to forget statistics and embrace life—and him!—with passionate energy. But for Ingrid, making such changes is painfully difficult ... *My Wild Irish Rogue* was written soon after Helen's own trip to Ireland, a land that clearly inspired her.

Carole Buck has done it again! Her latest romance, *Happily Ever After* (#350), has more than a fairy-tale ending; it's magical through and through, with all the wit and warmth that have made Carole such a popular SECOND CHANCE AT LOVE writer. The enchantment begins when Lily Bancroft dresses up as Snow White, hoping to wrangle money out of the quellingly authoritative, yet devastatingly masculine man known as the Lone Wolf of Wall Street. How she and Dylan Chase move from antagonism to ardor, achieving a poignant understanding—helped along the way by Dylan's playboy brother and Lily's lovably offbeat friends—forms the stuff of a marvelously inventive, deeply satisfying romance...

Finally, with the emotional power and sensitivity she's known and loved for, Karen Keast tackles one woman's hard-earned bitterness toward men in general and one male in particular. Reluctant Lauren Kane is certain that, if she lets him, sexy Nyles Ryland will become her sensual nemesis. Incorrigible Nyles is intent on proving the same thing—*but* he's gambling Lauren will learn that giving in to her feelings doesn't have to mean defeat, and that her treacherous heart can prove her gentlest ally. The result is *Tender Treason* (#351), a moving story of stormy suspicions, willful seduction, and oh, so sweet surrender.

I hope you enjoy all six of our July releases. And don't forget to drop us a line—we love to hear your thoughts and comments.

Warm wishes,

Ellen Edwards

Ellen Edwards, Senior Editor
SECOND CHANCE AT LOVE
The Berkley Publishing Group
200 Madison Avenue
New York, NY 10016

SECOND CHANCE AT LOVE™

CAROLE BUCK

HAPPILY EVER AFTER

A
SECOND CHANCE AT LOVE
BOOK

HAPPILY EVER AFTER

First edition published July 1986

First printing

Printed in the United States of America

Second Chance at Love books are published by
The Berkley Publishing Group
200 Madison Avenue, New York, NY 10016

- 1 -

GIVEN HIS YOUNGER brother's relentless enthusiasm for the juvenile, there was only one conclusion Dylan Chase could come to when he was informed that a character from a fairy tale was waiting in the reception area of the Chase Legacy Foundation.

Gary was playing a practical joke. Another practical joke. And *he* was the intended butt of this one.

Dylan stared at the intercom on his younger brother's chronically messy desk, trying to control his temper. "Snow White, Miss Mills?" he repeated. The words came out cold and edged, like shards of ice.

"Yes, sir," Gary's secretary replied hesitantly.

"Snow White is waiting at the reception desk." What next? The Wizard of Oz phoning from the lobby?

"Yes, sir," came the careful answer. "She . . . she says she has a nine o'clock appointment with Mr. Chase—ah, your brother, sir."

Dylan took a deep breath, clamping down on the

urge to remind the woman that he, too, had a nine o'clock appointment with "Mr. Chase."

He'd arrived for the appointment five minutes early, as was his habit. It was now nine-fifteen. That was twenty wasted minutes. As head of ChaseCo International, a multi-million-dollar conglomerate, time was one thing he couldn't afford to waste.

Damn! It wasn't as though he was looking forward to reading Gary the riot act again. Quite the contrary. But he didn't have a choice. Gary was one of the responsibilities he'd shouldered twelve years before, when a private-plane crash killed his father and grandfather, leaving him, at age twenty-four, in charge of the Chase family and its considerable fortune.

The burden—and the suddenness with which it had descended—might have crushed another man; but Dylan Chase had been born and bred to accept it. He'd been strong to begin with, and the exercise of power had made him stronger. As long as Gary needed carrying, he'd carry him.

Of course, Dylan was aware that his relationship with his younger brother had deteriorated in recent years. He and Gary had been very close once. But something—the decade-wide gap in their ages, perhaps, or the sharp divergences in their natures—had changed that.

In the beginning, they'd quibbled over little things such as the length of Gary's hair and his lamentable habit of dousing nearly everything he ate with ketchup. But they'd progressed to quarreling about Gary's barely passing academic record, his irregular employment performance, and his apparent refusal to take anything—including balancing his checkbook—seriously. What Dylan considered responsibilities, Gary rebelled against as restrictions. What Dylan saw as fecklessness, Gary viewed as freedom. There were times when Dylan felt that he and his younger brother were playing out Aesop's fable of the ant and the grasshopper: Dylan hoarding for a rainy day while Gary played . . .

And while Dylan had tried repeatedly to patch up their differences, he hadn't had much success. In an effort to seem a little less like the autocratic older brother, he'd arranged to have today's discussion in Gary's office rather than summoning him to his own. Unfortunately, his ploy not only hadn't worked, it had evidently been manipulated by his irresponsibly prankish younger brother to blow up in his face!

Gary had always had a certain fondness for the old exploding-cigar routine.

"Ah—Mr. Chase?" the secretary's voice asked through the intercom. Dylan speculated briefly on whether she was knowingly involved in Gary's little game—whatever that little game was. Somehow, he doubted it. Miss Mills sounded genuinely upset.

"What about the Seven Dwarfs?" he inquired with a flash of sardonic humor.

"S-seven Dwarfs?"

"Did Snow White bring her Seven Dwarfs?" he clarified. It would be a decidedly "Gary" touch if she had.

"Oh. Well—ah—I don't know . . . sir." Dylan's mouth twisted slightly at her tone. He could imagine how this conversation was going to be recounted in the ladies' room. "I—I'll ask the receptionist."

"Thank you, Miss Mills. You do that."

Snow White and the Seven Dwarfs. He shook his head. His six-year-old niece, Kerri, had recently referred to the story as "Snow White and the Seven *Divorces*." Given that her mother—Dylan's sister, Diana—was barely thirty and already in the sixth shaky month of her third ill-considered marriage, Dylan could understand how the little girl had made the mistake.

Of course, Diana was no Snow White. Although her

first husband, Kerri's father, could have qualified for the nickname "Grumpy." And husband number two definitely had been a contender for the title "Dopey." As for the current—

"Mr. Chase? There are no dwarfs. Elise the receptionist says she—Snow White—says they had to go off to work."

"No doubt they were singing 'hi ho, ho ho' when they did," Dylan murmured, more to himself than to the secretary. It appeared the unknown Snow White at least had the wit to stick to her character.

"Sir?"

Dylan glanced at his gold Rolex wristwatch, debating the pros and cons of a sudden impulse. Why not let Gary's little stunt run its course? Dylan could use a good laugh—even if it was on him. Besides, something about this fairy tale female piqued his curiosity. At the very least, he wanted to get a look at her.

"Tell the receptionist to send Snow White in, Miss Mills," he ordered.

"Send her—" the secretary cleared her throat. "You want to see her, Mr. Chase?"

"Yes." Dylan didn't say anything more. He knew he didn't have to.

"Right away, sir."

Dressing up as Snow White hadn't been Lily Bancroft's idea. Frankly she'd always considered Snow White one of the wimpier fairy tale heroines. Still, she'd gone along with the scheme, as she'd gone along with so many others during the last six and a half years, for the sake of the Potluck Playhouse.

That wasn't to say she wasn't having second thoughts about the plan. She was. In fact, she'd been having second thoughts ever since Paisley Stevens, artistic director of the Playhouse, had decided that the only way they were going to get the money they needed was to make a "unique" impression on the Chase Legacy Foundation. Somehow—and Lily had long since given up trying to figure out how this sort of thing happened—that relatively innocuous decision had been translated into her making the playhouse's funding pitch dressed as Snow White. Paisley had even spent fifteen minutes giving Lily her interpretation of Snow White's character and motivation.

Paisley had been ecstatic when Garrison Chase himself had called to make the appointment to talk about their application for funding. She'd raved about how approachable and interested he'd sounded. Lily, who generally handled the nitty-gritty of the playhouse's money-raising efforts, had been surprised and pleased, too. But she hadn't let herself get overly excited. And although she'd accepted the Snow White idea, she'd put her foot down when Paisley suggested that the Seven Dwarfs tag along as well, "for effect."

For effect. Oh, yes, she could imagine what "effect" the Seven Dwarfs would have had on the oh-so-proper ladies and gentleman of this obviously oh-so-proper Park Avenue philanthropic organization!

Lily would have slumped in her seat at this point, but the black cotton bodice of her costume was about a size too small, and she was afraid she'd split a seam—or worse. Folding her hands in her lap, she began to twiddle her thumbs.

Actually, all things considered, the outfit wasn't *that* awful. It was a very good copy of the Snow White costume in the famous Walt Disney cartoon classic, complete with a swirling calf-length skirt and cute royal-blue and scarlet puffed sleeves. Of course, the cute puffed sleeves were cutting off the circulation in her arms, and she had nine thousand hairpins drilling into her skull because Paisley had decreed that Snow

White could not go around with loose shoulder-length tresses. Still, it could have been worse. Paisley could've insisted she bob her light-brown hair and dye it jet black in the interests of authenticity.

Lily glanced around, tapping her black ballet-slippered toes against the slightly threadbare Oriental rug beneath her feet. She wondered how long she was going to have to cool her heels before being permitted to see Mr. Garrison Chase. She didn't particularly mind being kept waiting. It gave her a chance to run over her fund-raising pitch in her head one last time. She didn't even mind the weird looks she was getting from people; she'd gotten plenty of weird looks over the past twenty-eight years. What she *didn't* like was the atmosphere.

The decor in the place was the epitome of restrained good taste: rich wood paneling, warm chintz fabrics, solid but graceful antique furniture, and a pleasant collection of English land- and seascapes done by a variety of moderately well-known painters. But, as restful and graciously comfortable as the area seemed at first glance, its underlying aura was one of faintly snobbish superiority—of old, arrogant money.

Lily knew the ambience and the attitude well. She'd been unwillingly introduced to them one month after her tenth birthday . . . four days after the death of her parents. She'd spent ten miserable years existing—not really living—in a huge mansion that reeked of soul-stifling condescension. The mansion (she couldn't call it a home) belonged to her maternal aunt, Amanda Wilding . . . of the Boston banking Wildings.

It was something she would never—*ever*—go back to.

"Ah—excuse me?" the receptionist interrupted her reverie.

Lily's chin came up. She suppressed a wince as a hairpin dug into her scalp. "Yes?"

"Mr. Chase will see you now," the woman told her. "It's right down this hallway. The corner office."

Naturally, Lily thought a bit cynically. This is the Chase Legacy Foundation. Anyone named Chase rates a corner office.

"Thank you very much," she said, reaching for her oversized and overstuffed shoulder bag as she got to her feet. She gave the receptionist a smile and set off down the hall as directed.

Somehow, she resisted the impulse to hum "Whistle While You Work" as she went.

Dylan did three things in the ten seconds of silence that followed Lily's entrance into his younger brother's office. He stood. He stared. He smiled.

And then he said: "So . . . you're Snow White."

Uh-oh, Lily thought, feeling a little like a wild animal caught in the headlights of an onrushing car. Maybe I should have brought the Seven Dwarfs along after all.

This—this man was a *philanthropist?* Yes, he had the bearing and the manner. The air of absolute confidence that comes with blue blood and gilt-edged securities. And he certainly looked wealthy enough to have money to burn—much less give away to worthy causes. Lily was willing to bet that the faultnessly tailored navy suit that fit so well across his broad shoulders had been custom made on Saville Row. His white silk shirt and burgundy foulard print tie had a similar air of expensive elegance. She wouldn't have been surprised to learn that his shoes were made to order. But there was something more than that . . .

He was tall—two or three inches over six feet—and well built, with an athlete's balance and grace. His face was hard and tanned. It was all planes and angles, topped with a thick thatch of neatly styled mahogany-colored hair. There was a hint of sensuality in his well-shaped mouth. There was a hint of sensuality in his unusual amber-brown eyes, too, as well as a gleam of ruthless perceptivity and commanding intelligence.

He had the presence of a patrician-warrior . . . the boldness of a born leader. He was definitely not the man Snow White was dreaming about when she sang "Some Day, My Prince Will Come."

Until he smiled. And then . . . well, and then Lily's pulse started leaping around like a Mexican jumping bean.

Slightly appalled by her reaction, Lily squared her shoulders—carefully. The last thing she wanted to have happen in front of this disturbingly virile man was to have her relatively modest endowments burst out of what was beginning to feel like her extremely immodest bodice.

"Mr. Chase?" she asked, dredging up some of the social poise that had been drilled into her during a decade of seemingly endless deportment lessons. She didn't care how nice this man had sounded on the phone when he'd talked with Paisley; he was dangerous! And that killer smile he'd turned on: Was it something he practiced, or did it just come naturally? In either case, it should be registered as a potentially lethal weapon.

"That's right," Dylan nodded. He had to give her credit. That polite tone of inquiry was very nicely done. If he hadn't been dead certain this situation was another one of Gary's setups, he would have been convinced by it.

It *had* to be a setup! After all, Gary knew his reason for coming down here today was to discuss the increasingly outraged complaints the board of trustees had been making about the very motley collection of people and programs he'd recommended as potential recipients for foundation funding over the past year. Plainly, his younger brother had decided to counter outrage with outrageousness. But what was the punch line?

Unless . . . unless it was "Snow White" herself. God knew, something about her had hit him like a blow to the gut when she'd walked in.

Dylan couldn't remember ever having had this kind of irrational, instantaneous response to a woman. Not even during his hyperhormonal prep school years, when he'd spent a lot of time taking cold showers and trying to sublimate his sex drive in sports.

What was it about her that got to him? Was it the way her ridiculous costume accentuated the slim curves of her slender body? Or was it the way her toffee-colored hair was pinned up to reveal the graceful length of her neck and the slightly stubborn set of her chin and jaw? Or was it the imperiousness of her nose and the unplucked but strongly arched line of her brows?

And her mouth! Touched by some soft, rosy color, it wasn't quite in proportion with the rest of her features, but its ripe fullness was a study in temptation. As for her wide-set warm yet wary green-gray eyes . . .

Get a grip on yourself, he ordered. The woman is *not* for real! Gary probably hired her from central casting. So, just play along until you figure out what the hell is going on.

He smiled again. "You know, it's too bad you didn't bring the Seven Dwarfs with you," he commented. He was curious to see how she'd handle this gambit.

Lily told herself she should feel relieved, not weirdly resentful, that Garrison Chase seemed amused by her effort at creative fund-raising. Looking at that uncompromising, aristocratic face, she had the unpleasant sensation that the Snow White scheme could easily—and disastrously—have backfired. In fact, she had the feeling it could *still* backfire if she wasn't very, very careful.

She put on her most dazzling smile. "Oh, they were

looking forward to meeting you, too, Mr. Chase," she replied. She saw something flash in the depths of his eyes. She wasn't entirely certain what the flash signified, but she was positive it wasn't the birth of a charitable impulse. "But, as I told the receptionist—"

"They had to go off to work."

"Exactly. And even if they hadn't . . . well, the subway ride uptown would have been too much of a strain for them. Especially for Bashful. He's very sensitive."

Dylan stiffened. "You took the subway dressed like that?" he demanded, forgetting his previous advice to himself about staying under control. His eyes arrowed to the top of the faintly shadowed cleft revealed by her snug-fitting neckline. Was this woman crazy? Didn't she know what kind of an enticement she was? Looking the way she did—she'd actually ridden the New York City *subway?*

Lily stiffened, too, at the censorious note she thought she heard in the question. She'd endured a decade of having her every word, thought, and action dissected and disapproved of. She wasn't going to take any more of it! *Especially* not from a man she'd just met.

"Actually, Mr. Chase, I took a taxi," she informed him frostily. "Not that it's any of your business."

Dylan took a deep breath, shocked to discover that he had a sudden and inexplicable urge to tell her that it damned well *was* his business. Everything about her was his business, including who and what she really was and how she'd gotten involved in one of Gary's practical jokes.

What was going on with him? He didn't know her name, for heaven's sake, and yet he was feeling protective . . . no, *possessive* of her!

"Ah—why don't you sit down over here, Miss White?" he invited, reining in his runaway reactions. He came out from behind Gary's desk. "Or do you prefer *Ms*. White?"

Enough already, Lily decided. She didn't trust this man and she didn't trust her response to him. The sooner she got their interview on to a businesslike footing, the better.

"I prefer Miss Bancroft," she declared, walking forward. She offered him her hand politely. He took it and shook it briefly. His touch was sure, strong . . . and electric. Lily pulled back quickly, not wanting to find out what would happen if the contact was prolonged.

"Bancroft?" Dylan repeated, maneuvering her neatly over to a sofa and chair arrangement. With unthinking courtesy, he waited for her to sit, then followed suit. Now that they were near each other, he could smell her perfume. It had a delicate floral scent, spiked with an unusual note of spice. It suited her perfectly.

"Yes," Lily affirmed, looking him straight in the eye. "My name is Lily Bancroft, Mr. Chase." She didn't detect the slightest flicker of recognition. There was more than a flicker of something else in his gold-flecked gaze, however, and it made her very edgy. Why was she so aware of this man? It wasn't like her to notice whether a man's after shave suited him (his did) or whether a man was wearing a wedding ring (he wasn't). It wasn't like her at all! "I'm with the Potluck Playhouse—we specialize in theater for children."

"The Potluck Playhouse," he echoed, wondering who had come up with the name. He also wondered if the faint flavor of Boston he picked up in her speech was genuine of affected. Somehow, he was inclined to go with the former.

"That's right," Lily nodded, trying to clamp down on a sudden spurt of irritation at his manner. She reminded herself that she was on Chase turf, soliciting Chase money, and if this particular Chase wanted to pretend he had no idea who she was and why she was there, she'd just have to go along with it. In this situation, she had to play by Chase rules.

The problem was, Lily Bancroft had always had trouble adhering to other people's rules, particularly when those other people tried to use their wealth to command her compliance.

"And this playhouse is where?" Dylan inquired. Just how much of a background story had she and Gary cooked up?

"The East Village. On Second Avenue," Lily informed him, trying to keep her aggravation out of her voice.

"I see. And I take it you've come to discuss a grant application?" he probed. The prickly independence radiating from her was an intriguing twist. So was the bit about specializing in children's theater. Just where was this little scenario heading?

"Exactly, Mr. Chase." Suppressing a sigh, Lily dug hastily through her shoulder bag. As she did so, her fingers encountered the red Delicious apple Paisley had jokingly given to her the night before, to present to Garrison Chase at the start of their interview. It was a little late for that sort of gesture now, even if she'd been in the mood to make it, which she wasn't. In any case, she had the feeling that this man was the carnivorous type; he seemed more likely to take a bite out of her than out of a piece of fruit. Trying to quell her growing sense of uneasiness, she extracted some printed material. "This is a copy of the application we submitted to your foundation," she announced, handing him the papers.

Dylan rapidly flipped through what she had given him, absorbing the facts and figures he was reading with characteristic efficiency. The presentation looked extremely well-prepared . . . even professional.

Maybe a bit *too* professional? he asked himself with a sudden feeling of disquiet. Yes, Gary sometimes went to great lengths to set up his pranks, but this . . .

"Well?" Lily prodded, wishing she could figure out what was going on behind those amber-brown eyes. At least he seemed interested in what he was reading. His dark brows were drawn together as though he was genuinely concentrating. Lord knew, she'd spent enough time trying to make their application worth concentrating on.

Dylan flipped to the sheets of financial documentation, his sense of unease growing. Damn! The pages were more readable that most of the annual reports he had to wade through. "You seem to have a very good person doing your books," he observed, frowning.

"Ah—thank you," she said. It wasn't exactly the reaction she was looking for, but she was willing to take any positive feedback she could get. "Paisley Stevens's son, Sam, keeps track of our financial records." She did not think it was necessary to add that Sam was a gangly seventeen-year-old whose main hobby was speculating —with remarkable success—in commodities futures.

"Paisley?" Dylan felt slightly better. Paisley was exactly the sort of name Gary would pick out.

"She's the playhouse's artistic director," Lily said. "Ah—it says Patricia Stevens on the application, but no one ever calls her that. She used to be a Broadway gypsy. A dancer. Paisley was her stage name. Only then she hurt her knee. That's how she met her husband. He's an orthopedic surgeon and she went to him for a consultation. But Tom didn't operate, he married her. Paisley quit dancing and went back to college. She got a degree in child psych with a minor in theater. Eventually, she got involved with a program for bringing the performing arts to underprivileged kids. The Potluck Playhouse evolved out of that."

Either this is the most elaborate joke Gary has ever devised, Dylan thought, or you have completely misjudged—and misled—this woman. You'd better find out which, *now*.

"And . . . how do you fit in to all this, Miss Bancroft?"

"Well, about seven years ago, my husband Howie broke his foot—"

"Your husband?" Oh, God, no! She was married?

Lily blinked, offended by his tone. "Yes, my husband. Howard Davis, Junior."

"You don't use his name." It was an accusation. Dylan temporarily shoved aside his determination to find out what was going on. He wanted to find out about *her*. *All* about her.

"I'm divorced!" she snapped.

There was an awkward pause. "I see," he said after a long moment.

No, Lily thought, he didn't. Very few people saw—much less understood—her three-year marriage to Howie Davis of Springfield, Massachusetts. Looking back, she realized she hadn't understood it either; at least, not until it was over. And once she'd acquired the maturity to understand the impulses that had led her into the relationship, as well as the self-destructive paths they might have impelled her to take, she could only say a prayer of thanks for her ex-husband.

"Miss Bancroft?" Dylan cut in, watching the play of emotions over her fair-skinned face. What was going on? Maybe things had gone far enough. Maybe he should simply put his cards on the table.

Oh, yes, terrific idea, Dylan, he mocked himself instantly. If she *is* part of a joke, she won't admit it. And if she isn't—

If she isn't, she'll probably storm out of here and you'll never see her again.

"Miss Bancroft—" he began heavily.

"Yes, *Mr. Chase?*" she countered. Lily was fed up with this man and the unsettling impact he had on her. She made her displeasure plain by adopting the coolly condescending tone her Aunt Amanda had often used on her. Lily had tried to adapt to her aunt's perfectionist standards; she truly had. But, even at ten years of age, she had been too much her own person to be forced into a mold that didn't suit her. And the Wilding family mold had emphatically not suited her.

It hadn't suited her mother, Jessica, either.

Dylan stared at her. She sounded like one of those stiff-rumped society dowagers his mother was always having over for tea.

"Yes, Mr. Chase?" Lily repeated, her green-gray eyes icing over.

"Ah . . . I'd like to hear more about the Potluck Playhouse," he said, deciding to go back to letting the situation develop—or unravel—of its own accord. He also made up his mind that if her pitch was genuine, he'd see that she got her funding.

Lily said nothing, trying to gauge whether or not his interest was real. It was very difficult to read this man. All her impressions were distorted by her flowering awareness of her own femininity. It was an awareness *he'd* made blossom.

"Please?" he prompted, giving her a flash of the knee-weakening smile he'd turned on at her entrance. "You must have quite a commitment to the project to . . . ah . . . do what you do." His eyes ran over her.

Lily swallowed, feeling as though he was touching her. A few strands of her hair had worked loose and were curling down the back of her neck. She raised a slightly trembling hand and patted them back into place. "You—you're talking about my coming here dressed up as Snow White, I take it."

"Among other things." Was she or wasn't she? He couldn't make up his mind. He shifted toward her. Again, he caught the evocative fragrance of her sweet-spice perfume.

Lily decided to lay things on the line. She took a deep preparatory breath, then exhaled slowly. "Look, Mr. Chase," she began carefully, meeting his gaze evenly. "I know how this sort of foundation operates. I know how many applications for funding you receive, how many deserving people you interview." Lily did know, firsthand. Amanda Wilding had her fingers in many philanthropic pies, and she'd made certain that her niece learned that the business of charity was just that: business. *Big* business. "We—Paisley Stevens, me, everyone associated with this—we didn't want the playhouse to get lost in the shuffle. It means too much to us. To our neighborhood. To the children. We wanted to come up with a way to stand out from the crowd. So . . ." she debated with herself for a moment before continuing with complete honesty. "Paisley did some checking around, and you have a reputation for being receptive to unorthodox approaches," she concluded. She moistened her suddenly dry lips with a dart of her tongue and waited for a reaction.

For a moment, Dylan forgot about the possibility that all this might be leading up to some Garyesque punch line. He was fascinated by the changes in her eyes. The color of her irises seemed to mirror her mood: The more intense it became, the greener they turned. He wondered what happened when she was aroused. "That's . . . very interesting," he returned, stirred to provocation by the direction of his thoughts. "But are you sure your information about my reputation is correct? I've always felt I was receptive—or, perhaps I should say responsive—to unorthodox *women*."

Lily felt herself quiver under the voluptuous stroke of his voice. The earlier amber hardness in his gaze had melted into an expression that made her pulse start to pound. She didn't need to look down to know her breasts were straining against the bodice of her Snow White costume in a way Walt Disney never would have allowed. She also knew that the presence of the Seven Dwarfs wouldn't have offered her any protection against this man. The arrival of the Seventh Cavalry, maybe . . .

"Mr. Chase—" she began, moistening her lips again. There was no mistaking the intention in his face. Just how far are you willing to go for the sake of the Potluck Playhouse, Lily? she asked herself. And just how far do you want to go for *yourself?*

"Lily—" He was going to kiss her. He'd wanted to kiss her from the moment she'd walked into Gary's office. He'd probably get his face slapped—or worse—but he was willing to risk it for a taste of that soft, ripe mouth. And, after he kissed her, he was going to straighten this situation out.

He'd probably end up getting his face slapped for that, too.

His fingers cupped her chin and Lily allowed him to coax her face up. The intensity of his gaze shook her and she half-closed her eyes against it, lashes fluttering as her lids came down. She heard him whisper her name and felt the warm fan of his breath as he began to lower his mouth . . .

The kiss never came.

"Dylan!"

Dylan stiffened as though he'd been hosed down with ice water. Releasing Lily, he glanced sidewards, instantly registering that the door to the office had swung open and his younger brother had just walked in.

His first thought was a furious jump to the conclusion that he had, after all, been had by some stupid setup. His second was that there was no way in the world Gary could feign such a completely convincing expression of surprise, disbelief, and embarrassment.

Dylan swore once and muttered his brother's name.

Lily, whose eyes had flown open as soon as she'd felt the change in Dylan's body, ignored the epithet. It was the second thing he'd said that nailed her attention like a railroad spike. *"Gary?"* she repeated, her gaze going back and forth between the man next to her and the one who had just come in. She could see any number of physical similarities, although the man making his entrance was about ten years younger, a bit slighter, and far more casually dressed than the other. In some ways, he was more conventionally handsome, too, with his easy, open features. Yet there was a softness—almost a weakness—about him. Where the man who had been on the verge of kissing her was utterly male, utterly adult, this newcomer was still something of a boy.

"Dylan—I didn't expect to find you still here," the younger man said in a strange voice. His brown eyes swept over Lily. For a moment, his expression was speculative to the point of offensiveness. Then it changed radically and he slapped his forehead. "Oh, my God!" he exclaimed. "You're the woman from the kids' theater—the Potluck Playhouse! I completely—oh, look, I am sorry. I got so excited about your application last week that I called your director—ah, Parsley? No, Paisley!—and set up an appointment myself. I didn't remember to tell my secretary so she could put it on my calendar and I totally forgot. I feel—What can I say?"

Dylan had gotten to his feet during this stumbling speech, a combination of anger and plain old sexual frustration roiling up in him. He opened his mouth to speak, but Lily cut him off.

"You, I take it, are Garrison Chase," she said, standing up very, very slowly. She was shaking.

"Guilty," Gary conceded, moving forward. "And you're—ah—Lily Bancroft, right?" He extended his hand. "I can't tell you what a jerk I feel like," he said sheepishly.

Lily ignored the outstretched hand and the implied apology. She rounded on Dylan, snapping her head so violently that several hairpins went flying. "Then *who,"* she demanded through clenched teeth, "are *you?"*

"Dylan Chase," Dylan answered. "His brother." He paused for a second, waiting for a reaction. There didn't seem to be any. "Lily—"

That got a reaction. "Don't you *dare* call me Lily!" she exploded. "Don't you dare call me *anything!* You—you—Just where do you get off pretending to be somebody else, hmm? I mean, what did you think you were doing? I came here today in good faith, Mr. Dylan Chase. And I came here for a very important reason. To try to get funding for something I believe in!"

"I realize—"

"Do you? I seriously doubt that!" she spat at him furiously. "What did you think? That because I was willing to make a fool out of myself by dressing up as Snow White, you were free to make a fool out of me yourself? Is that what you thought?"

"No, of course not," Dylan returned, his own temper flaring. "I thought—"

"I don't care what you thought!" she raged back. "Just who the hell do you think you are, anyway?"

There was a distinctly dangerous silence. Gary, who'd made a remarkable recovery, was the one who broke it. "Well, I don't know who Dylan thinks he is," he offered blandly. "But the title on his engraved business cards reads chief executive officer of ChaseCo International."

Lily paled. "ChaseCo—" she faltered, then stopped

as a number of things fell into place like the clichéd ton of bricks. Sam Stevens, who tracked the careers of Manhattan moguls the way other teenage boys followed the exploits of famous athletes, had mentioned Dylan Chase and ChaseCo. "You're the man with all the money! The—the—" she scrambled for the phrase. "The 'Lone Wolf of Wall Street.'"

No wonder he hadn't seemed cut out for the role of professional philanthropist! This man acquired wealth; he didn't give it away. And to think there had been a few moments when she'd actually been *attracted* to him. The idea appalled her. She knew Dylan Chase's type far too well. He was the kind of man her Aunt Amanda had often pointed to as being a suitable mate for a Wilding heiress. Well, thank God, she wasn't a Wilding heiress anymore!

"Miss Bancroft—" Dylan began again, deciding the wisest course was to opt for the more formal form of address. He acknowledged that she had a right to be angry. But he had the sense that there was something more than this one specific misunderstanding fueling her outburst.

"It's not really fair to say Dylan has *all* the money," Gary interrupted with the air of a man who had given the matter great thought. "Our mother inherited some. And Diana—she's our sister—got some, too. And, of course, I have my share as well. But Dylan *is* the head of the family. . ."

"So he has the power of the purse," Lily finished grimly.

Dylan said nothing as he saw the cold distaste in her expression. Yes, there was something more than this single situation at the root of her sudden hostility. But what? Had that husband of hers—Howie—been some kind of rich, overbearing bastard?

"Pretty much," Gary agreed airily. Of the three people in the room, he was the most at ease. "And, since the purse keeps getting bigger, my big brother Dylan keeps getting more powerful."

"Gary, that's enough," Dylan gritted out suddenly.

"Yes, it is," Lily said. She stuck up her chin and threw back her shoulders. She fixed Gary with a sharp look. "If you were serious about being excited by our funding application, I'd like to schedule another appointment. With *you* . . . through your secretary."

"At your convenience," Gary said immediately.

"Thank you. And as for *you*—" she glared at Dylan for a few seconds before inspiration struck. Reaching into her shoulder bag, she pulled out the apple Paisley had given her. She flung it at Dylan without a word of warning. Fortunately, his reflexes enabled him to catch the piece of fruit before it hit him in the face. "I hope it's full of worms, *Mr. Chase!*" she announced acidly. Then she turned on her slippered heel and stalked out.

- 2 -

DYLAN'S FIRST IMPULSE was to go after Lily, to force her to listen to his explanation of what had happened, and then to kiss her senseless. Fortunately, rationality intervened before he could act on this primitive inclination.

I'll let you go, Lily Bancroft, he thought. For now . . . but not for long.

Then he confronted Gary.

"Too bad she didn't bring the Seven Dwarfs, huh?" his younger brother commented mildly, sauntering over to him. "Do you mind, Dyl?" Gary went on, plucking the apple out of his hand and taking a huge bite out of it. "I didn't have time for breakfast." He chewed, swallowed, and turned on a cheeky grin. "Hey, what do you know! No worms!"

"If memory serves, Gary," Dylan returned, feeling an all-too-familiar combination of exasperation and affection. "If memory serves, Snow White's apple had poison in it. Not worms."

Gary chomped down on another bite. "Wishful thinking, big brother?" he jibed, then pulled a considering look. "Let me guess. You figured I was trying to stick it to you with one of my justifiably notorious practical jokes and she was part of the setup for the gag, right? Only instead of letting on, you decided to play along and maybe turn the tables. Am I close?"

Dylan's mouth twisted. "It's too bad you don't occasionally turn your powers of deduction to something useful."

"Why should I bother? You're useful enough for both of us." Gary chewed for a few seconds before continuing. "But, never mind that. In case you have any lingering doubts, the lady is exactly who she said she was. She's for real."

"And all that about the meeting you'd set up?"

Gary grimaced. "God, you are suspicious sometimes, Dylan. Look, when you called me Friday and informed me we were going to have a little chat in my office at nine A.M. on Monday, I honestly didn't remember I already had an interview with Lily Bancroft on my calendar. You may have a mind like a steel trap, but I don't. I just forgot. So, sue me."

"And did you 'just forget' about our appointment, too?" Dylan consulted his Rolex. "Is that why you came in so late this morning?"

"I didn't forget, no. I was late because of traffic."

"Traffic! You live three blocks from here. You could crawl to work on you hands and knees and still make it on time."

"I was coming in from the Hamptons. I spent the weekend out there," Gary explained offhandedly. "Although, to tell the truth, I really wasn't in any hurry to get into the city for our tête-à-tête. I mean, I've still got the singe marks from your last verbal blasting. Remember? The one you gave me when I told you I wanted to quit the foundation and travel around for a few months?"

"Were you intending to show up at all?"

Gary sighed and shrugged. "Hey, I figured you'd get here five minutes early, kick around in my office till ten after nine, maximum, then burn Pam Mills's ears off dictating a scathing memo to me and split."

Dylan shook his head ruefully. "If it hadn't been for the intervention of Snow White, I probably would have done just that," he acknowledged. "And, speaking of Snow White—"

"You want her address and phone number?"

"I have them." Both had been on the application, and Dylan, unlike his brother, had an extremely retentive memory.

"O-o-h-h-h?" Gary dragged the syllable out.

Dylan ignored the obvious innuendo. "I want the Potluck Playhouse application approved," he said flatly. It was the least he could do for Miss Lily Bancroft.

Which was not to imply that that was *all* he was going to do for her. No, Dylan could and would do more. Much more.

Gary's brows went up. "I see. Well, your wish is the board of trustees' command around this place."

"Good."

Dylan's younger brother clicked his tongue. "You know, I almost wish I could take the credit for what happened here this morning," he mused.

"The *credit?*"

"Yeah. I always pictured myself as a matchmaker. And, judging by what you and the lady were on the verge of doing when I walked in, I'd say you were pretty well matched."

Dylan didn't disagree. Instead, he glanced at his watch again.

"Duty calls?" Gary inquired.

"Doesn't it always?"

"No time to chew me out for my sins, huh?"

Dylan studied him silently for several seconds. Yes, they had been friends once—very good friends, despite the difference in their ages and temperaments. "I have . . . more important things to do," he said abruptly, and headed for the door.

"Hey, Dyl?"

He checked his step and turned back. An instant later, Gary lobbed the half-eaten apple at him. Dylan caught it deftly.

"It's yours," Gary explained with a brief grin. "And if you're trying to come up with a way to apologize to her, I suggest a dozen roses and something tasteful from Tiffany's. It never fails for me—and I've had a *lot* of practice at apologizing to women."

Dylan smiled crookedly, a gleam of anticipation appearing in his eyes. "I have the distinct impression that where Lily Bancroft is concerned, 'never fail' formulas don't work."

He punctuated this assertion by taking a bite of the apple.

"Snow White Versus the Lone Wolf of Wall Street," Paisley Stevens intoned, pretending to be reading off a theater marquee. "I have to tell you, Lily. It has a certain ring to it."

Lily, Paisley, and Paisley's son, Sam, were sitting in the cluttered cubbyhole designated as the Potluck Playhouse's business office. The room contained four mismatched chairs, two battered desks, and a rack of costumes from several previous productions. The walls were covered with theatrical posters.

"It's not funny," Lily insisted, irritably shoving several fistfuls of tawny hair back over her shoulders. One of the first things she'd done when she'd returned to her loft apartment—located over the playhouse—from her uptown appointment had been to change out of her Snow White outfit and let her hair down. "The man *is* a wolf, you know. The adjective *predatory* definitely applies to him." So did the adjectives *infuriating, arrogant, deceitful . . . attractive . . . sexy . . .*

"I wish I'd gone with you," Sam Stevens spoke up suddenly, looking up from the stack of receipts he was shuffling through with the finesse of a Las Vegas blackjack dealer. Although Lily had given his mother an angrily detailed account of what had happened, he'd insisted on hearing the whole story for himself when he'd shown up at the playhouse after school, as he did every Monday. "I'd love to get to meet Dylan Chase. Heck, I even would've dressed up as one of the Seven Dwarfs."

"My six-foot son—a dwarf?" Paisley teased, running her fingers through her short curly hair. Mother and son both had red hair and gray eyes. But while the forty-one-year-old Paisley was petite, creamy-skinned, and moved with fluid grace, Sam was tall, freckled, and ambled around as though he'd been stuck together with chewing gum and baling wire.

The teenager rolled his eyes. "Hey, Mom, I made a pretty convincing *turkey* in that Thanksgiving pageant a few years back, didn't I? If I can do a turkey, I can do a dwarf." Looking at Lily, he inquired: "You think *you* had a rough time dressed up as Snow White? Try going to the bathroom in a turkey suit! The stupid zipper got jammed up with feathers or something—" He shook his head. "Anyway, back to Dylan Chase. Geez. The man is one of my personal heroes. I mean, even if he did act like a sleaze this morning, we are still talking about a financial giant here, you guys. A *major* financial giant."

"We could be talking about a major financial *problem,* Sam," Lily reminded him unhappily, propping her chin in her palm. Her heavy hair swung forward. "In case you don't recall, we need this grant. And, thanks to Mr. Dylan Chase's warped sense of humor, we probably won't get it!"

"Lily, don't be so negative," Paisley advised. "You said yourself the other one—Garrison—was willing to give you another appointment. You said he said he was impressed by our application."

"Yeah," Sam chimed in. "And you said Dylan Chase thought that the person you've had doing the playhouse's books has been doing a good job." He preened a bit. "I like it. I like it."

"Maybe," Lily said. "But I don't like Dylan Chase. I don't like what he did. I don't trust his type. I don't trust *him*."

"You barely know him—" Paisley began to protest.

"I know him, Paisley. Believe me, I know him. He'd get along wonderfully with my Aunt Amanda. They both have so much money and so much power they think they can do just exactly what they want, when they want, to whom they want." She made a swift, silent vow that Dylan Chase wasn't going to do anything to her . . . *ever*.

"Well—" Sam Stevens seemed sobered by Lily's tone. "If the playhouse doesn't get the grant, we'll just have to put off the renovation work for another year."

"And pray the building code inspectors don't come around," his mother added with a grimace.

Lily sighed. "If we don't get the grant, I can probably talk to the bank—" She didn't want to, but she would.

"No!" Paisley declared flatly, her gray eyes flashing. "Lily, you did more than enough for the playhouse when you bought this building with that insurance annuity or whatever it was you got from your parents' death."

"I needed a place to live."

"You could've bought a luxury co-op with a view of Central Park for what you spent."

Lily shrugged. "Luxury doesn't mean a lot to me, Paisley." It hadn't meant much to her mother, either. Jessica had grown up surrounded by the best of everything money could buy, but she'd gladly thrown it all away to elope with Mark Bancroft, a struggling artist of modest means and an equally modest background. Except for an inheritance from a maternal relative, she'd been cut off from the Wilding fortune after her marriage. She and Mark had used the money to set up a trust for Lily. That had meant they'd had to live on a shoestring budget, but it hadn't mattered. Jessica and Mark had been rich in love, and they'd endowed their only daughter with an affectionate and independent spirit before their tragic early deaths in a car crash . . .

"You won't even charge the playhouse a reasonable rent, for heaven's sake!" Paisley was saying. "Look, Lily, I know you've got access to Wilding money—even if your Aunt Amanda did her best to disown you when you married Howie. But I also know you've told me you wouldn't touch that money with a ten-foot pole."

"Not for myself. But for the playhouse—"

"No," Paisley repeated. "I won't let you do something like that."

"You let me go uptown to make a fund-raising pitch dressed as Snow White," Lily reminded her.

"That's different."

There was a brief silence. During it, Lily reflected on how lucky she was to have a friend like Paisley Stevens. Paisley understood her aversion to the Wilding money and all it represented.

"Look, the playhouse isn't in that bad shape financially," Sam said with characteristic practicality. "Like I said, we can't afford the renovations, but the place isn't going to go under . . . unless, or course, Mom's new production crashes and burns at the box office." He made this last comment with a mischievous twinkle.

Paisley fixed her only child with a maternal glare. "Samuel John Stevens, *Sleeping Beauty in Space* is *not* going to crash and burn at the box office!" She glanced at Lily. "You've read the script, Lily—"

"Oh, it definitely won't crash and burn," Lily agreed immediately. "I only wish you hadn't substituted a slime monster for the wicked fairy. Do you have any idea how much ooze we're going to have to clean up after each performance?"

Paisley gave her a limpid smile. "I don't clean up, I'm the director."

"Just be glad Mom didn't call for any live animals this time out, Lily," Sam advised with a chuckle. "Oh, hey! I almost forgot. You know this laser light thing Anthea says she wants?" Anthea was the mother of a ten-year-old girl who attended workshops at the Potluck Playhouse. A successful avant-garde artist, she'd volunteered to design the sets for *Sleeping Beauty in Space*. Her plans were quite spectacular—and ingeniously inexpensive.

"If anything's going to crash and burn in this production, it's Anthea's laser light thing," Paisley said.

"No, seriously, Mom. I asked around at school, and there's a couple of guys who think they can rig up something really amazing."

"These aren't the same couple of guys who got arrested for rigging up something to record what went on in the girls' shower room, are they?" Lily inquired. The "school" Sam had referred to was a private one for the intellectually gifted.

"Nah," Sam replied, shaking his head. "Anyway, Croaker and Thad didn't get *arrested*. Geez, they're only thirteen. They got suspended. I heard the CIA wants to hire than as some kind of consultants on electronic surveillance. Anyway, about this laser thing. If you can arrange it to be some kind of official independent-study project through the school—"

He broke of as a buzzer shrilled, signaling that there was someone at the back delivery entrance.

"Now who could that be?" Paisley asked, lifting her brows.

Lily got up. "There's only one way to find out. You two settle Anthea's 'laser thing.' I'll be back in a minute."

It took her considerably longer than a minute. First, she had to undo a multitude of locks. Then she had to struggle to get the heavy rusty-hinged door open. When she finally succeeded, the sight that confronted her rendered her speechless with surprise for nearly thirty seconds.

A pair of pleasant-faced, neatly-uniformed delivery men stood patiently outside, their spotlessly polished delivery truck parked behind them. The older of the two had a faintly officious air and carried a clipboard. The younger was bearing an absolutely exquisite crystal vase filled with a dozen fragile bunches of lilies of the valley.

Lily blinked, pushing her glossy curtain of hair back out of her face and making a tugging adjustment in the sunshine-yellow pullover she was wearing. "Yes?"

"Miss Bancroft?" the elder delivery man asked.

"Yes," she affirmed, her heart starting to pound with alarming rapidity. It couldn't be! But who else—? "I—I'm Lily Bancroft."

"These are for you, ma'am. If you'll just sign here, please."

"Ah—thank you." Like an automaton, Lily signed.

She then received the flower-filled vase. The crystal was cool and sensuously smooth against her palms and fingers. The heady scent of the lilies of the valley teased her nostrils. Nestled in among the tiny white blossoms and vivid green stems was a cream parchment envelope addressed to *Miss Lily Bancroft* in a bold but disciplined hand. "Who—" she managed to get out as the delivery men turned away.

"You'll have to read the card, ma'am," the older one said.

She had to set the gift down while she wrestled the door closed and locked it once again. She would have read the card there and then, but the light was too dim. Besides, every feminine instinct she had told her that the handwriting on the envelope could only belong to one man.

"—these guys are practically pros, Mom," Sam was saying earnestly when Lily walked back into the office. "They'll be—*holy geez,* Lily!" he exclaimed, his gray eyes widening.

"Holy geez, Lily, is right," his mother echoed as Lily set the vase down very, very carefully. "Lilies of the valley in *September?* Who in heaven's name sent them?"

"That," Lily said, plucking the envelope out of the flowers with unsteady fingers, "is what I'm going to find out."

"You definitely don't get something like this at Woolworth's," Sam observed thoughtfully, staring at the vase.

"It's Steuben glass," Lily said, opening the envelope.

"What's Steuben glass?" the teenager wanted to know.

"It's what the President sometimes gives visiting heads of state," his mother informed him.

"Wow."

Lily was inclined to agree with this assessment after scanning the hand-written note inside the envelope. She felt herself flush slightly.

"Lily?" Paisley asked.

Lily cleared her throat. "'Dear Miss Bancroft,'" she read aloud. "'I apologize for my behavior earlier today. I assure you my actions were very much out of character. (No, Snow White, I am not the Big Bad Wolf in disguise.) Please accept these flowers as a sign of my sincerity and please allow me a chance to explain. Dylan Chase.'"

There was a pause. Lily glanced from the note to the flowers and back again. Damn the man! Not only had he managed to make an incredibly graceful apology, but he'd done so with a style—to say nothing of a disarming flash of wit—that made it virtually impossible for her to refuse to forgive him. And Lily didn't want to forgive Dylan Chase for anything: not for his actions earlier in the day, not for attracting her, not for being who and what he was. She wanted to stay angry . . . she wanted to stay away from him.

"To quote my son again," Paisley said finally, "*wow*."

Lily dropped the note onto the desk. The fine cream vellum stationery seemed absurdly out of place amid the clutter. "It's a very nice gesture," she declared, feigning an indifference she was far from feeling. "A very nice, very expensive gesture. The sort of gesture somebody like Dylan Chase can afford."

"Lily!" Paisley frowned. "A 'very nice, very expensive' gesture would have been having his secretary call some florist to order a dozen roses. Lilies of the valley in Steuben glass with a hand-written note is a couple of light-years away from that."

Lily hooked her hair behind her ears, nibbling her lower lip moodily. Thrusting her hands into the pockets of her jeans, she rocked back and forth on her feet. Her fundamental sense of fairness forced her to concede Paisley's point—much as she hated to. The flowers and the note were something special. Something... sensitive. And sensitivity wasn't something Lily expected in a man like Dylan Chase.

A man like Dylan Chase. Are you so sure you know what kind of man he is? a little voice inside her head asked.

Oh, yes, I'm sure, she answered back fiercely. Aunt Amanda started pitchforking the Dylan Chases of the world at me the day I turned eighteen!

"Lily?" Paisley repeated.

"You're right, of course," Lily said quickly, trying to hide how unsettled she was. "I'm being bitchy. I suppose I should write him a note saying I accept his apology. Maybe I—" She broke off as the phone rang. Because she was the closest, she picked it up. "Potluck Playhouse," she answered in a businesslike tone.

Dylan Chase recognized her voice instantly—with his body as well as his brain. Once again, he registered the faint flavor of Boston Brahmin in her inflection. "Miss Bancroft? Dylan Chase."

For a few seconds, Lily felt a lot like the heroine of *Alice Through the Looking Glass*—thoroughly disoriented. She knew both Paisley and Sam were staring at her curiously. "Mr. Chase," she got out. Not bad for a start. An octave or so higher than usual, but not bad. She cleared her throat. "Mr. Chase, we were just talking about you," she went on. Her tone was a little syrupier than usual, but it was back to an acceptable register.

Dylan heard the pseudo sweetness with mixed feelings. Obviously, the note and the flowers hadn't completely mollified the lady. He hadn't really expected they would. On the other hand, she hadn't slammed the phone down on him, something he'd halfway anticipated she might do as soon as she heard his voice.

"'We?'" he echoed. "You and a few of the Seven Dwarfs?"

"Me and some of the people from the Potluck Playhouse."

"Ah."

Lily glanced at Paisley. The older woman was mouthing something at her. She didn't need to be a lip reader to catch the gist of the message. "I want to thank you for the flowers," she said. "They're . . . beautiful. And the vase is lovely, too."

"I'm glad they pleased you." His voice was low, almost caressing.

"I . . . I appreciated the apology."

"Do you accept it?"

"It would be hard not to," she admitted after a moment.

The reluctance—no, the wariness—in her voice disturbed him. "Lily—"

"I accept your apology," she said quickly.

"Dylan."

"What?"

"I accept your apology, *Dylan,*" he instructed. "Calling me by my first name will keep you from getting me confused with the other Mr. Chase."

"Somehow, I don't think that will be a problem now that I've met both of you," she retorted. Garrison Chase had seemed like a very nice young man. Dylan Chase, on the other hand . . .

Nice was not the word—the flowers, vase, and note notwithstanding. But Dylan Chase was definitely a man . . . *all* man.

"Would you care to expand on that?" Dylan asked. He'd picked up on the sarcasm in her riposte, of course. But there had been something else, as well.

Suddenly, illogically, he was positive that whatever had hit him when he'd first seen her, she'd felt it, too.

"No, I wouldn't," Lily returned flatly, shutting her ears to the provocative invitation she thought she'd detected in his question.

"According to the newspaper, you don't have a performance tonight. Would you like to have dinner with me?"

"I—*no!*" The nerve of him!

Dylan wasn't surprised by the blunt refusal. He wasn't particularly troubled by it, either. "As I said in my note, I'd like a chance to explain my behavior. After that—" he let his voice drop, putting a deliberate edge on his words. "We can talk about your grant application to the foundation."

For a split second, Lily came close to exploding. Then she realized she was being baited. "Blackmail, Mr. Chase?" she countered.

He laughed "If that's what it takes to get you to say yes to my dinner invitation," he told her frankly.

Lily remained silent for several moments; not because she was angry, but because she was fighting an inexplicable urge to share in his humor.

"Lily?" Dylan wished he could see her face.

"I'll . . . I'll have dinner with you on two conditions," she said finally.

"Just two?"

"Number one, I pick the place."

"Fine." Mentally, he braced himself for the worst cuisine New York City had to offer. A fast-food joint, probably.

"And two, we go Dutch. You pay your way. I pay mine."

There was an undertone of warning in the way Lily said this. Dylan filed it away for future reference.

Money again. The lady was very, very touchy on the subject. "Dutch it is," he agreed. "Your address is the same as the playhouse's?"

"Yes."

"I'll pick you up, then. Shall we say eight, Lily?"

"Let's say eight-fifteen . . . Dylan."

Lily was waiting on the sidewalk underneath the playhouse's marquee when Dylan's chauffeured, black limousine pulled up at precisely eight-fifteen. She'd debated for a long time about what to wear before settling on a narrow cinnamon wool skirt and a high-necked cream cotton blouse trimmed with crocheted lace. The blouse had been a bargain find at a shop that specialized in antique clothing. A loosely woven mohair shawl in shades of copper, tobacco, and ivory was draped casually over her shoulders as a guard against the cool night air. Her long caramel-brown hair was coiled into a knot at the nape of her neck. Except for a pair of pearl earrings, she wore no jewelry.

Lily walked forward slowly, the heels of her brown pumps clicking softly against the pavement, as a nattily uniformed driver got out of the car and opened the door for Dylan.

"Quite a transformation," Dylan commented after they'd exchanged polite greetings. His amber-brown eyes roamed over her in lingering appreciation, taking in the graceful dignity of her bearing and the unconscious sensuality of her movements. The timeless yet distinctly individualistic elegance of her clothing appealed to him. So did the spirited intelligence in her wide green-gray eyes and the promising ripeness of her lightly glossed mouth.

"I only wear my Snow White costume when I'm going uptown," she told him. Dylan was dressed in the same impeccably tailored navy-blue suit he'd had on when they'd met that morning. She was struck again by the aura of carefully leashed power he projected. She was also acutely aware of the stirrings of her slender body in response to his slow visual appraisal.

"I see," he responded with a quick, vivid smile. He then nodded at his chauffeur. "Lily, this is my driver, Rodgers. Rodgers, this is Miss Bancroft."

"Rodgers." The chauffeur appeared to be in his mid-fifties. He was of medium height and build and carried himself with military erectness. His close-cropped hair was steel-gray and his hatchet-sharp features were schooled into an unreadable expression.

"Miss Bancroft." He touched the brim of his hat politely.

Dylan watched the exchange with interest. Although there was no one thing he could point to as proof, he had the immediate impression that Lily Bancroft was—or at least had been, at some time in her life—accustomed to dealing with servants. "Have you decided where you'd like to go?" he asked.

She tilted her head a little, pretending to think. The blandness of his inquiry told her that he was expecting some outrageous choice. "Well . . ." she let her eyes skate over the limousine. "I hadn't realized you were going to bring a car," she remarked sweetly. "You know, I've always had a yen to go through a—oh—a Burger King drive-in in one of these."

Bingo, Dylan thought. While he wasn't about to delude himself that he'd completely figured out Miss Lily Bancroft—much less the compelling attraction he felt for her—he was beginning to get a line on how her mind worked.

If Lily hadn't been watching for some reaction, she might have missed the brief gleam of triumph in Dylan's eyes and the lightning-swift look he traded with his driver. She thought she saw a fractional relaxation in

Rodgers' poker face. And there was definitely a hint of amusement in the sudden quirking of Dylan's well-shaped lips.

"What?" she demanded, glancing back and forth between the two men.

"I had the feeling you might be harboring a longtime yen for drive-in food," Dylan explained, not bothering to pretend that he didn't understand what prompted her question. "So, I asked Rodgers to check into the location of some of the nearest fast-food places."

"Oh." That's one to you, Mr. Chase, she decided without rancor.

"It's a bit of a drive, Miss Bancroft," Rodgers said. "I believe I did find one Burger King out on Long Island . . ."

"No, that's all right, Rodgers," she smiled. "I wouldn't want to put you to any trouble." The delicate stress she placed on the second-person pronoun strongly suggested that her consideration for Rodgers did not extend to his employer. Lily looked at Dylan. "There *is* a punk-rock sushi bar round the corner you might find interesting," she remarked with an angelic smile.

"Let me guess. They rip the raw fish apart with their bare hands?" Interesting, indeed. He wondered what she would say if he told her that he didn't give a damn where they ate as long as they did it together.

"Something like that," she agreed. There was a dangerous, distinctly male glint in his eyes that aroused equal parts of anticipation and apprehension in her. Lifting one hand, she patted her hair, chiding herself for her uncharacteristic coyness. "Actually, though, there's a good Italian place a few blocks from here. Guido's and Angelina's. We could walk." She glanced at Rodgers. "You could give Rodgers the night off."

"The *whole* night?" He couldn't resist.

You left yourself open for that one, Lily, she informed herself tartly. "Unfortunately, I turn into a pumpkin at midnight," she said evenly.

"We'll have to do something about that," Dylan declared smoothly. "All right. Guido's and Angelina's it is." He looked at his driver to make certain he'd heard the name of the restaurant. After getting a tiny nod of acknowledgment, he went on: "That will be all for tonight, Rodgers. Thank you."

"Sir," Rodgers nodded once more. "Miss Bancroft."

"Good night, Rodgers."

- 3 -

"WELL, DO YOU approve?" Lily asked, taking a sip of wine.

Dylan allowed himself a moment to savor the mouthful of *pollo alla carciofi*—sautéed chunks of chicken with peas and artichoke hearts—he had just swallowed. The entrée, like the rest of the meal, had arrived at their table unordered. "It's delicious," he said without exaggeration. This hole-in-the-wall restaurant might not offer much in the way of decor beyond checked tablecloths and candles in wax-dripped Chianti bottles, but the food it served was terrific. "Does it always work like this? With the customer getting whatever the kitchen cares to serve up?"

Lily smiled. She'd wondered how he'd react to the way things were done at Guido's and Angelina's. "Customers get menus. Friends of the family get whatever Angelina decides is best for them."

"I see." There was no doubt in his mind that Lily was a "friend of the family." She'd been greeted at the door by Guido himself, who'd treated her like a long-lost daughter. Then she'd introduced Dylan, who'd found himself on the receiving end of the *padrone*'s sharp-eyed assessment. Luckily, whatever Guido had seen, he'd apparently approved of it; after fifteen seconds, he'd stopped staring, smiled, and shaken Dylan's hand.

Lily forked up a piece of artichoke. "Does it bother you? Not being able to order what you want, I mean." Her tone was half-serious, half-teasing.

Dylan studied her for a moment. "I like making decisions for myself," he said. There had been some awkwardness between them at the start of the meal, but once Lily had listened to—and apparently accepted—his explanation of his earlier behavior, they'd gotten on very well. Their conversation had been light, and spiced with laughter as he'd regaled her with stories about several of Gary's more outrageous pranks. But there had been undercurrents . . . unsettling, intriguing undercurrents.

"And for other people." The statement was casually made, but faintly edged. Lily wasn't trying to start a quarrel. She simply knew she had to keep reminding herself of who this man was—of *what* he was. She was acutely aware of how drawn she was to Dylan Chase; she had to do something to keep him at a distance.

Dylan remained silent for a few seconds. "I have responsibilities, Lily," he told her quietly, thinking about his family . . . and about the family business.

"But you do like being able to order what you want."

The amber-gold cast of his eyes turned a smoky topaz. "I like being able to *get* what I want," he corrected, his voice sliding down a few notes. "But it's not always a matter of ordering. Sometimes . . . I ask." He took another bite of the chicken dish, enjoying the taste and the texture of the food with slow, sensual pleasure. His gaze never wavered from Lily's face.

She had to glance away. Her hand wasn't quite steady as she lifted her napkin and dabbed at her lips. Oh, yes, she could imagine how this man "asked" for what he wanted. She could imagine so well that she felt a sudden tautening of her breasts and a sweet rush of sensation lower down . . .

She scrambled mentally for the conversational equivalent of a cold shower as she forced herself to meet his eyes again. "Ah—have you always lived in New York?"

Dylan smiled fleetingly. He was experienced enough to know precisely how he was affecting her; he was honest enough to admit that she affected him the same way. "I was born and raised here," he said. "but I went to prep school and college in Connecticut."

"Choate and Yale?" she guessed after a second.

"Hotchkiss and Yale." The glow from the candle flickering on the table gilded her fair skin and was reflected, dancing, in the depths of her green-gray eyes.

"And then . . . mmm . . . Harvard Business School."

He nodded. "You sound as though you think you've got me neatly pigeonholed," he observed. He had the impression she didn't particularly like the pigeonhole.

"If the shoe fits . . ."

"What about you?" Dylan leaned forward slightly.

"Given a choice, I prefer to go barefoot," she parried.

He took a swallow of wine. "You aren't a native New Yorker," he observed.

"I grew up here and there," Lily said with a little shrug. The Bancrofts had moved around a lot when she was young. She hadn't minded; for her, "home" wasn't a *place* . . . it was a state of mind that depended mainly on the loving presence of her parents.

"Including Boston." It wasn't a question.

"Including Boston," she confirmed, giving him an inquiring look.

"There's a trace of 'Hahvahd Yahd' in your voice," he said, explaining his deduction.

"Oh."

"Did you go to school in Boston?"

Lily's educational background included a stint at one of the most exclusive girls' boarding schools in the country and two years at Radcliffe, but she was not about to tell Dylan Chase that. "I dropped out of college to get married," she said.

"To . . . Howard Davis, Junior." Dylan didn't need to search for the name; it was burned into his memory. He was aware that she'd avoided answering his previous question, and he wondered at the evasion. But he was willing to let the subject drop in order to find out about her ex-husband.

"That's right." Lily chased a pea around on her plate with her fork. The intensity of his interest made her uneasy. The shadowy illumination in the restaurant seemed to emphasize the aristocratic austerity of his features, throwing the arrogant jut of his cheekbones and the thrust of his jaw into strong relief. He looked extremely formidable.

"Is he in the theater, as well?"

Lily's lips curved into a small smile. Dylan was pigeonholing her, too. "He's an executive with his family's appliance-manufacturing firm in Massachusetts," she said. It was odd how things had turned out. Howie's decision to run off to New York City with her had been as much an act of rebellion as her decision to marry him had been. Yet, in the end, he'd conformed to his family's expectations, and, as far as Lily knew, he was perfectly happy doing so.

"Appliance manufacturing?" Dylan didn't try to hide his surprise.

Lily eyes sparkled. "Well, actually, Howie was a stand-up comedian when we were married," she conceded.

Lily could still recall, in great detail, how her Aunt Amanda had reacted to *that* bit of news. She'd been appalled, which had been just fine with Lily. She'd barely entered her teens when she'd recognized that little—if anything—she did pleased her exacting, unbending relative. So, with the perversity of adolescence, she'd set out to *dis*please her aunt as much as possible. Her marriage to Howie Davis had been the pièce de résistance in that campaign.

Dylan took a moment to digest this information. "I take it he wasn't successful."

Lily stiffened. "He didn't make much money at it, no," she answered flatly. Indeed, she'd supported both of them with a variety of part-time jobs. It hadn't always been easy, but she'd reveled in her escape from anything and everything connected with the Wilding family and had fully enjoyed the assertion of her independence.

Dylan's mouth tightened. Why the hell was she so touchy? He hadn't been implying—

Well, perhaps he had been. In Dylan's world, success was very much equated with money. And power.

"Was he funny?" he asked quietly, carefully.

Lily thought she heard an oblique apology in the question. She also experienced a moment of dismay at her own defensiveness. Her expression softened, then blossomed into a crooked smile. "Yes, Howie was funny," she said. "Not really show-biz funny—if you know what I mean. He never learned how to be 'on.' And he had some problems with stage fright." Her laughter was full of affectionate memories. "But he *was* funny. He made me laugh so much. I think . . . I think that's why we stayed together for three years. We had the same sense of humor."

Dylan let a few seconds pass. Instinct told him she was being honest with him. He sensed there was still a great deal she wasn't saying; but what she *was* telling him was the truth. "Why did you break up?"

Lily's long lashes came down, veiling her eyes. The curve of her mouth was reflective. "I . . . we didn't exactly break up," she said slowly. "It was more a matter of . . . of . . . growing up. Of growing apart." She looked across the table at Dylan. "But we're still friends," she concluded simply.

There was a pause in their conversation then, as their waiter appeared and began deftly clearing their table. Once that was done, he served their dessert—a liqueur-laced compote of fresh fruit accompanied by a sinfully rich assortment of macaroons.

"What about you?" Lily inquired after the man moved away. She nibbled on one of the pastries.

"I've never been married," Dylan replied. There was a tiny crumb of cookie on her full lower lip. He had to fight down the urge to lean across the table and kiss it off.

"Did you ever come close?" Lily was genuinely interested. She also preferred to ask the questions rather than answer them.

Dylan shook his head. There had been a number of women in his life, of course; but his relationships had always been based as much on mutual convenience as mutual pleasure.

"Mmm." Lily was quite sure that Dylan Chase was unattached by choice, not because of any lack of opportunity. And, somehow, she didn't like to consider how many "opportunities" he might have had.

Dropping her eyes, she spooned up a cherry from her dessert dish. She was acutely conscious of how intently Dylan was watching her, of how his gold-flecked gaze kept stroking over her mouth. Despite the sweet juiciness of the fruit, her lips seemed suddenly dry. She moistened them with an unthinking dart of her tongue.

Dylan took a steadying breath, wondering where his self-control had gone to. He wanted Lily Bancroft. The desire he felt for her was a throbbing, tangible thing. And what astonished him was the recognition that she wasn't trying to attract him. Dylan had been chased by enough women—most of them subtle, all of them stylish—to have a working knowledge of just about every feminine wile in the book. If Lily had any wiles, she sure as hell wasn't using them on him.

"Scusi." Guido suddenly materialized by their tucked-in-a-corner table. *"Per favore.* You are *Signor* Chase, *si?"*

"Ah—yes. *Si.*" Dylan responded. He wasn't certain if his reaction to the interruption was gratitude or aggravation.

Guido gave Lily an apologetic look, then turned his attention back to Dylan. "There is a telephone call for you," he said. "A business problem." He made the announcement with an edge of outrage.

"Business?" Lily echoed, visibly puzzled. "But how—?"

"Rodgers passed on the name of the restaurant to someone on the ChaseCo switchboard," Dylan explained tersely, getting to his feet. "I'm sorry, Lily. This won't take long."

Lily nodded her understanding, the ruthless determination of his last four words chilling her a little. Her initial impressions of him reasserted themselves and she felt a flash of sympathy for the person who was calling him—to say nothing of the person who was responsible for the "business problem."

The call took four minutes. Exactly four minutes. All Lily could think of when Dylan returned to their table was the all too descriptive nickname someone had hung on him: the Lone Wolf of Wall Street.

"You've got to go," she said quietly. It wasn't a question.

"Yes." There was a crisis in the making in Hong Kong. He'd been anticipating problems; recent currency fluctuations had warned him trouble was brewing, and he'd already made contingency plans. Unfortunately, the delicate, opening stages of those plans required his direct, undistracted supervision.

Dylan had learned a number of important things from his father and grandfather. One of the most important was: If the work is really dirty, do it yourself.

"Lily, I am sorry," Dylan said. It wasn't a *pro forma* courtesy. There had been other nights, with other women, when he'd been thankful for the intrusion of business. This wasn't one of those nights and Lily Bancroft wasn't one of those women. "But some heads need to be knocked."

"And you're the one who needs to knock them," Lily finished, trying to sort out her feelings. She supposed she should be relieved by this interruption. It underscored—far more effectively than the reminders she had been giving herself—who and what Dylan Chase was.

"Yes." Damn! The wariness was back in her eyes. Dylan could feel her distancing herself from him as surely as if she'd started backing away physically. But why? Instinct told him her reaction wasn't simply a matter of injured female pride over his making business his first priority in this situation. There was more to it than that. But *what?*

"Guido doesn't take credit cards," Lily said as he pulled out a thin black calfskin wallet. "Or personal checks."

Dylan paused. He'd gotten out of the habit of carrying much cash. "I see."

Lily bit her lip, hoping he didn't think this was a ploy to embarrass him. "I should have said something before," she told him. "I'm just so used to how Guido and Angelina do things that I didn't think—I'll get the check."

Dylan lifted his brows. "I thought we'd agreed this was going to be Dutch treat," he reminded her mildly, swiftly acquitting her of trying to one-up him in some way.

Lily smiled. "I think I can trust you to repay me for your share."

He smiled back. "With interest."

They walked back to the theater together, their hands brushing occasionally. Lily's strangely oversensitive body registered and retained the electricity of each fleeting touch. By the time they reached the playhouse's marquee, she had the feeling she was about to start giving off sparks.

"You—you'll probably have trouble hailing a cab in this neighborhood," she said, tilting her chin up as she faced him. "Do you want to come inside and call—"

"There's a car on the way." The sweet-spice scent of her perfume assailed his nostrils. The cool autumn air had brought a rosy color to her cheeks. "Lily . . . I want to see you again."

She let a moment go by. "And you like being able to get what you want," she returned, a glint of emerald in her eyes. "Don't you, Dylan?"

He recognized that she was quoting his own words back at him. "Yes," he replied with devastating simplicity. "I do." His mobile, sensually shaped lips twisted. "Lily, I can't *order* you to see me again—"

"But you can ask." There was the faintest hint of flirtation in her voice, the first Dylan had heard that evening. There was also a distinct flavor of uncertainty. Plainly, Lily hadn't made up her mind about him.

"Oh, I will ask," he promised. Lifting his hand, he gently traced the graceful curve of her cheek. Her skin was very smooth against his fingers. Several silken strands of her hair had worked loose and were blowing across her face. He tucked them back behind her ear in a gesture that held more than a trace of possessive intimacy. "The evening wasn't supposed to end like this," he told her, the look in his amber-brown eyes as frank as his tone of voice.

Lily trembled for an instant, then went still. Her pulse had started racing like the motor of a car at the start of a Grand Prix as soon as he'd begun caressing her face. "Dylan—" she whispered. "Dyl—"

He kissed her. His mouth poured over hers like hot wax. Melting. Fusing. Possessing.

Dylan had fantasized about the taste of her lips. They were sweet . . . with a slight flavor of the liqueur-laced fruit she had eaten for dessert clinging to them. They parted slowly in response to the coaxing pressure of his tongue.

Lily quivered a little as she felt him deepen the kiss. His mouth was firm and flexible as it moved over hers . . . exploring, exciting, enticing a response she found herself only too eager to give. She lifted her arms, her palms sliding over the strength of his shoulders and around his neck. Her fingers wove themselves into his hair.

One of his hands had moved to cup her jaw, controlling the angle of her face, giving himself increasing access to her mouth. The slightly callused ball of his thumb teased at the corner of her lips. His other hand had traveled slowly, sinuously, down the length of her body. It now rested, fingers splayed, on the gentle swell of her hip.

Whether by instinct or intent—or by some erotic combination of both—Dylan found the key to her senses and imprinted himself upon them. Willing or not, and Lily couldn't say for sure which she was, she absorbed everything he was offering. It was as though the essence of him was being injected into her bloodstream. The potency of it flooded through her. She sighed, her lips moving to shape his name.

Finally, Dylan lifted his mouth from hers and stared down at her. His expression made Lily tremble. He was looking at her as though he'd found something he'd always been searching for, only to discover that that something wasn't what he'd expected.

Without thinking about why she wanted to do it, Lily brought her hand around to touch his face. His jaw fretted once as she let her fingertips trail lightly over the raspy beginnings of new beard growth on his cheek.

She had the dizzy, dangerous feeling that her expression at this moment was a lot like his, and that frightened her. Dylan Chase was not what she'd always been searching for. In many ways, he was what she'd been trying to escape from for the past eight years.

"Lily—" Dylan sucked in a deep breath. He could feel her starting to resist him again. One step forward. One step back. Damn! What was going on behind those changeable eyes of hers? "The evening wasn't supposed to end like *this,* either," he said after a second, his voice a little husky. Out of the corner of his eye, he spotted a black limousine coming down the street toward them. Reluctantly, he let her go.

Lily had seen the car, too. She stepped back. The night breeze fluttered one fringed end of her mohair shawl. "You mean we weren't supposed to kiss good night?" she asked, bringing the shawl under control. It was a pity she couldn't do the same with her physical responses to Dylan Chase. Her voice might be reasonably steady, but her knees were as wobbly as unset gelatin.

"We were supposed to kiss . . ." he replied, deliberately leaving the statement unfinished. The limousine pulled up to the curb beside them, its motor purring. Dylan glanced instinctively at his watch.

Time is money? Lily wondered with a trace of acid. "Is it late?" she asked aloud.

"Ah—" Dylan realized that he hadn't actually registered the hour. He checked his watch again. "Eleven forty-five," he answered. "I'm sorry I won't be around to see you turn into a pumpkin," he went on, referring to the comment she'd made earlier. "Maybe next time?"

Lily looked at him. "Maybe," was all she said.

The next time she saw him was two days later, shortly before five P.M. She was coming out of the prop room, grubby and grumbling, and nearly crashed into him.

"Dylan!" she exclaimed, dropping the wrench she'd been carrying with a noisy clatter. She was unprepared for the surprised delight she felt at his unexpected appearance.

"Hello, Lily," he responded, warmed by the unforced pleasure in her sudden smile of greeting. Although he'd thought they'd parted on good terms Monday night, he hadn't honestly been certain of what kind of welcome —if any—she might give him.

He was very much the well-dressed executive in his impeccable gray pinstripe suit. His male elegance made Lily unusually aware of her own untidy appearance. While she had a very feminine appreciation of good clothes—plus the height and taste to wear everything from the classic to the kooky—Lily didn't normally give a lot of thought to the way she looked. Right now, however, she strongly wished she had the ability to transform her water-logged sneakers, patched jeans, and paint-spattered *A Chorus Line* sweatshirt into a more attractive ensemble.

"I—ah—what are you doing here?" she asked, hastily brushing her right hand against her thigh. She extended it, slightly dirty palm and all. "You didn't go to the matinee, did you?"

He took her offered hand and shook it briefly, fighting the urge to retain possession of it. "I'm afraid I missed this afternoon's performance of *Hansel and Gretel Go Hollywood,"* he replied. He wondered if she had any idea that her overlarge sweatshirt had slipped off her left shoulder in a very sexy fashion. Or if she realized that the haphazard way she'd pinned up her shiny brown hair made his fingers itch to pull it free. "But, I must say, the title sounds intriguing."

Lily laughed. "The show's intriguing, too."

"You obviously don't go in for the traditional approach to fairy tales. I saw the poster for your next production in the lobby. *Sleeping Beauty in Space?"*

"Paisley's philosophy is that we've got to give old stories new twists if we're going to keep the kids coming back. After all, we're competing against music videos, Saturday-morning cartoons, movies filled with special effects. Children are very sophisticated, you know."

"Indeed, I do," he said with a smile. "My niece, Kerri, sometimes seems to be six-going-on-sixteen. Not too long ago, I overheard her singing 'Like a Virgin' by Madonna. She knew all the words. Of course, I didn't have the nerve to ask if she knew what all of them *meant*."

Lily laughed again. "I can't imagine you lacking the nerve to ask any woman—much less a six-year-old girl—anything," she joked. "But, to get back to my original question. What brings you downtown?"

"You," he said frankly.

"Me?" Brevity might be the soul of wit under most circumstances; however, in this instance, Lily felt it was the soul of provocation. She flushed slightly.

"I owe you a debt, remember?" He reached into the breast pocket of his suit jacket and removed his wallet.

"Oh—*that.*" She accepted the crisp bills he handed her. They crackled as though they were fresh from the mint. "Thank you," she said as she tucked them into her jeans.

"So—what have you been up to?" he asked.

"Well, I haven't been masquerading as Snow White—as you can probably tell," she responded, gesturing at herself.

His well-shaped lips—the firm male lips that had evoked such a powerful response in her only two days before—quirked. "You do look a bit like you might have been digging in the mine with the Seven Dwarfs."

"I wish! I've been wrestling with a leaky pipe in there for the past ninety minutes." She nodded back toward the prop room.

Dylan bent suddenly and retrieved the tool she'd dropped when she'd first caught sight of him. "A *wrenching* experience, I take it?" He gave her back the wrench.

Lily laughed for a third time, her eyes sparkling. "Another pun like that and you'll *get* it," she warned.

Dylan grinned unrepentantly. "You know, I recall your telling me over dinner that you're the assistant-everything here at the playhouse," he told her. "But I don't think you mentioned you're the resident handyman, too."

Lily gestured with the wrench. "Yes, well, there's some debate about how handy I am," she conceded. "The man who sold me this place told me it needed some work. He just didn't say how much."

"You *own* this building?" Dylan picked up sharply, his brows coming together.

Lily wanted to kick herself. Very few people were privy to the information she had just inadvertently let slip. She had never intended Dylan Chase to be one of them.

"Lily?" he pressed. Damn it, no, she wasn't going to clam up on him!

She sensed his determination and gave into it. "Yes, I own the building," she confirmed shortly.

He studied her narrowly. "It—it's an unusual type of investment property," he observed, probing through the opening she'd given him. The place was decidedly run-down. He'd seen plenty of evidence of that during his brief visit. And it wasn't exactly in the high-rent district, either. On the other hand, the building seemed basically sound and was attractively designed. Plus, the surrounding neighborhood bore all the signs of the first stage of an invasion by young, upwardly mobile professionals. In any case, as Dylan well knew, Manhattan real estate did not come cheap.

Lily could practically hear him making calculations. The next thing she knew, he'd be asking where she got the money to buy the building. She had no intention of talking about that. "Look, I live here," she said firmly, glancing upward to indicate the loft. "And I work here. Beyond that, I care very deeply about what goes on here. I care about the people . . . about the Potluck Playhouse. This building represents a commitment to me. Not an investment."

Dylan recognized a door when it was shut in his face.

He also knew sincerity when he heard it. He didn't understand—at least, not yet—why Lily wanted to keep her ownership of this building a secret, but he was willing to respect her desire for privacy on the basis of the passionate caring he read in her eyes.

"I . . . see," he said very quietly.

Lily blinked. She had the strangest sense he just might be telling the truth. The barrier she had slammed between them lowered. "Would you—would you like a tour of the place?" she asked. The smile she gave him was as much of an olive branch as the invitation.

"I'd like that very much," he returned. "And, afterward, maybe we can get a quick bite to eat? I know you've got another show here tonight. And I've got a plane to catch. But we've got time for—oh, say—a Whopper at Burger King."

Lily smiled, picking up on his reference to Monday night's little scene with Rodgers the chauffeur. "Sounds good to me," she said.

They actually ended up at a local delicatessen. It was the sort of place where the counter clerks alternated between abusing newcomers who were slow to place their orders and cosseting regulars with extra helpings of cole slaw and dill pickles. It was also the sort of place where the contrast in Lily's and Dylan's appearances passed completely unnoticed.

Talking over their sandwiches—pastrami for her, roast beef for him—Lily discovered they shared a passion for Alfred Hitchcock movies, modern art, the British Museum in London, and chocolate chocolate chip ice cream. She also discovered they shared a dislike of people who were obsessed with physical fitness, answering machines with pseudo-clever messages, and anchovies.

And, when their meal came to an end, she discovered they shared a very real reluctance to say good-bye to each other.

Two days later, she found out they also shared a liking for jazz . . . and baseball.

They met, purely by chance, at the Village Gate on Bleecker Street.

Lily had gone to the well-known club with Paisley and Tom Stevens. It had been a spur of the moment outing. Lily had suggested the idea to Paisley following the evening's performance of *Hansel and Gretel Go Hollywood*. Paisley, who had a dancer's appreciation for any type of good music, had quickly agreed and called her husband to join them.

Dylan, who had spent fourteen hours of the previous day locked up in meetings in Los Angeles and God knew how many hours of this one bucking turbulence on a flight back from the Coast, had come down to the Village on impulse, too. He was familiar with the quartet playing at the Village Gate, and their cool-yet-hot music struck him as the perfect prescription for relaxation. He'd gone out alone, although he'd tried to reach Lily by phone before leaving his Fifth Avenue duplex.

He told her as much when they'd spotted each other inside the club. They'd chatted casually for a few moments. One thing had let to another, and Dylan had found himself sitting at a table for four instead of by himself.

"I've heard *so* much about you, Mr. Chase," Paisley declared for openers. Lily, sitting next to Dylan, smothered a groan. Her friend was obviously in one of her postperformance "up" moods, and that meant mischief.

Dylan took the redhead's measure and grinned. "Dylan," he corrected. "I won't bother to ask what you've heard or who you heard it from. Just tell me: Am I allowed to plead the Fifth, or shall I just lie and deny everything?"

"You're something of an idol to our son, Sam," Tom Stevens commented easily. He was a calm, pleasant-faced man in his mid-forties. Lily knew him as a dedicated doctor, a reliable friend, and a stable counterweight to Paisley's volatile nature.

"Oh?" The name Sam triggered something in Dylan's mind. After a moment, the connection clicked into place. He glanced at Lily. "That's the Sam who does the playhouse's books?" he asked her.

"Ah—yes, that's right," Lily said, surprised at his memory. She'd only mentioned Sam to him once, after all.

Dylan nodded, then turned back toward Paisley and Tom, who were sitting across the table. "In that case, I'm flattered I have his good opinion. From what I've seen of his work, I'd say he has a lot of ability. I take it he's a CPA?"

There was a brief silence. Lily saw Tom and Paisley trade amused looks. Obviously, Tom had heard the story of her first meeting with Dylan from his wife. Equally obviously, the couple was going to leave the explanations about their gifted son to her.

"Actually, Dylan," Lily said wryly, "Sam's a seventeen-year-old high school senior."

Somehow, given the impression he'd formed of Lily's life, Dylan didn't find this at all odd. "Do you think he'd be interested in a summer job with ChaseCo?" he inquired without missing a beat.

"Seriously?" The question came in a three-part chorus from Tom, Paisley, and Lily.

"Seriously."

"He'll be down to sign up tomorrow," Paisley asserted.

They continued talking easily until the musicians started playing once again. Dylan leaned back in his seat. He was powerfully, yet very pleasantly, aware of Lily's closeness. She was humming softly, her long, loose hair swinging a little as she kept time with small movements of her body. Her thigh brushed against his now and again.

Letting the complex rhythms of the music take hold of her, Lily glanced at Dylan from beneath partially lowered lashes, trying to analyze exactly why she felt so attracted to him. It was no one thing she could pin down. The tug was just there . . . like a force of nature.

She was still mulling over his appeal when the leader of the quartet announced the foursome was taking a short break. Caught up in her thoughts, she lent only an absent ear to the conversation that sprang up between Paisley, Tom, and Dylan. Consequently, she was never sure how the subject of baseball came up. By the time she surfaced from her troubling reverie, the topic was already well launched.

"I—I'm sorry, Tom," she apologized, realizing Paisley's husband had asked her a question she'd completely missed. "I'm afraid I was tuned out for a few minutes."

"Tom wanted to know if you knew that Dylan played outfield in high school," Paisley informed her.

"Oh." Lily blinked. "No, I didn't." She turned toward Dylan. "You never mentioned that."

"And I'll bet you never mentioned you're an outstanding shortstop," Tom remarked.

"No, she never did," Dylan confirmed. He hadn't missed Lily's preoccupation. What had she been thinking about? he wondered. Whatever it was, her thoughts hadn't been altogether happy ones.

"Well, I wouldn't say I'm *outstanding*—" Lily quibbled, brushing her hair back behind her ears. She had a sudden premonition about where all this was heading, and she wasn't certain she liked the destination.

"Don't be modest, Lily," Paisley admonished. "She's one of the stars of the B and B league, Dylan."

"B and B?"

"Baseball and brunch," Lily explained. "Tom here recruited me a few years ago."

"Since which time," Paisley picked up, "my husband has wisely decided that diving headlong into second base to beat out a squeeze play isn't such a terrific idea for a middle-aged man with a bad back."

"Middle-aged?" Tom challenged in mock anger.

His wife winked at him. "That's not to say you haven't found other things to dive headlong into," she teased, then looked back at Dylan. "Sam's in the league now. They play the third Sunday of every month, May through October."

"I thought the playhouse has Sunday matinees."

"Oh, it does," Paisley nodded. "But I can't deprive the league of one of its stars, so Lily gets game days off."

"Say, Dylan," Tom began with a friendly, guy-to-guy grin. "What kind of shape is *your* back in?"

"Tom—" Lily began to protest.

"My back's just fine, Tom," Dylan grinned back.

"You want to play a little ball on Sunday? Sam was saying something the other day about the league being short a few players this month."

Amber-brown eyes sought and found green-gray ones.

"Well," Dylan drawled, "I think that would depend on whether or not I get to play on Lily's team."

- 4 -

LILY HAD EXPECTED that Dylan would be a good softball player. Given his lean, well-toned muscularity and innate male grace, it was obvious that he was a natural athlete who kept himself in excellent condition. What she honestly had *not* expected was that he would adapt almost immediately to the free-for-all spirit of the flagrantly unofficial Sunday baseball and brunch league. It was plain, at least to her, that Dylan Chase's standard operating procedure in any competitive situation was to play to win. She was surprised to discover that he was capable of playing simply to have fun as well.

Several of the other players recognized him even before she made the required introductions. The "league" boasted a stockbroker, two lawyers, and a *New York Times* reporter—as well as a Broadway choreographer, a translator for the United Nations, and the co-owners of a thriving health food store—among its members.

Dylan handled the recognition—and shrugged off the speculative looks—with casual charm. He even handled the irrepressible Sam Stevens, who, despite his wild enthusiasm for the summer job offer, seemed to consider it his duty as an opposing player to heckle Dylan each time he came up to bat.

Dylan's method of handling the gangly seventeen-year-old was to hit a pair of doubles, a triple, and a home run.

"Don't you find all Sam's chatter distracting?" Lily asked curiously at the end of the fourth inning as their team took to the field after scoring three more runs. She was still having a little trouble adjusting to the idea that the laughing, apparently carefree man striding along beside her was the same man who had earned the nickname the "Lone Wolf of Wall Street."

Dylan chuckled. "Sam's chatter is nothing compared with some of the verbal flak I've had to take at stockholders' meetings," he informed her.

"No, seriously—" She could hardly believe how open and accessible he seemed. He was wearing a baseball cap cocked at a rakish angle and his hair was boyishly ruffled. There was a smudge of dirt on his left cheekbone. One of the knees of his pelvis-hugging jeans had been ripped in a wild but well-timed slide into home plate during the previous inning.

"Seriously?" He grinned at her, his teeth showing white against his tanned skin. God, she looked good to him! She was ridiculously, ravishingly appealing in her crooked Mets baseball cap, baggy Snoopy sweatshirt, and skin-tight jeans. And those orange sneakers! He grinned again. "Okay. *Seriously.* Sam Stevens doesn't bother me one bit. You, on the other hand, have a very disruptive effect on my concentration."

"Me?" Lily's eyes widened and she looked down at

herself. "You've got to be joking!"

"Lily—" Dylan slipped an arm around her slim waist, pulling her close as he dropped his voice. "Do you have any idea what you look like from the rear when you do that little wiggle at the plate?"

"Dylan!" she admonished him. She wished she wasn't so conscious of the tingles dancing up and down her spine as their bodies bumped. "Hasn't anyone ever told you you're supposed to keep your eye on the ball, not on—uh—"

"Your backside?" he suggested, patting her bottom for emphasis. The denim-clad curves of her trim derriere fit his palm perfectly.

She jerked away from him. "Oh, go play in the outfield!" she retorted, manufacturing a show of outraged dignity.

Dylan doffed his own baseball cap and swept her a mocking bow. "With pleasure, my dear Miss Bancroft," he said. "With you playing shortstop, the view from center field should be very stimulating." He winked, relishing the flare of emerald in her eyes. "Especially with all those grounders the other team seems to be hitting."

Thanks to "all those grounders," Lily committed three unforced errors during the remaining innings. She told herself it was just a coincidence.

As it turned out, her sudden and uncharacteristic inability to field a ball didn't make much of a difference. Lily's team won. Not officially, of course. No one ever "officially" won or lost a game in the Sunday baseball and brunch league. Still, there was a considerable amount of *un*official gloating going on as the players adjourned to the converted loft over the Potluck Playhouse where Lily lived.

Brunch lasted, very pleasantly, very informally, into the late afternoon. Because Lily had generously overestimated the amount of food she'd need, most of her guests departed carrying leftovers. Sam Stevens, who'd demolished six bagels, eight ounces of cream cheese, and a half-pound of smoked salmon before guzzling down a gallon of fresh-squeezed orange juice, allowed himself to be coaxed into taking home an entire strawberry cheesecake.

"Whew," Lily exhaled with half-feigned, half-real relief as she shut the door on the last guest. After throwing the deadbolt, she turned to survey her apartment—and to face Dylan Chase.

He was sprawled comfortably on the huge sectional sofa that dominated the living room area of her large and airy loft. He looked perfectly at home in the casual, cluttered setting. His head was supported by a pair of slightly threadbare midnight-blue velvet pillows, and his bare feet were propped up on the edge of the brass-hinged rattan chest she used as a coffee table.

"You throw a good brunch," he complimented her, his half-lidded eyes wandering over her in leisurely assessment. She'd exchanged her Snoopy sweatshirt for a loose-fitting sweater in peachy-pink cotton. Watching the soft, subtle movements of her breasts, he wondered if she was wearing a bra.

Lily smiled, slowly combing her fingers through her hair. "Thank you." The three-button collar of his pullover top was completely undone, revealing a triangle of tanned skin at the base of his corded throat. His faded jeans seemed to be clinging to his lean hips and sinewy thighs even more intimately now that he was sitting down. "And . . . I appreciate your help." Dylan had, unbidden, assumed the role of host during the brunch; and he'd done it so naturally that Lily had accepted the situation before she consciously recognized what was going on. "You mix a mean Bloody Mary."

"One of the benefits of an Ivy League education." He

stretched and gave her a devilish grin. "So, we're alone at last," he observed, patting the cushion beside him invitingly.

Lily walked forward slowly, stopping a few feet away from him. "Don't get too relaxed, Mr. Chase," she advised after a moment. "Since you're the only one left, you're going to have to help me clean up."

"I'm yours to command, Miss Bancroft," he returned with faintly exaggerated gallantry. "But not just yet."

Changeable green-gray eyes met very steady amber-brown ones. Lily waited—waited, not hesitated—about ten seconds. Long enough to underscore, in her mind at least, her basic independence. Then she moved to the sofa and sat down next to him.

"I like your loft," he remarked after a brief, companionable silence.

"Do you?" Lily glanced around at her surroundings with a sense of satisfaction. While the funky eclecticism that characterized the place would probably give an interior decorator fits—and definitely offend her Aunt Amanda's conservative sensibilities—it spelled home to her. Every stick of furniture, every bit of clutter, had a story.

"Mmm. Especially the rainbow." He tracked the path of the vivid multihued striped that flowed up one wall, curved across a section of the ceiling, and arced down into the corner by the bathroom door. "And I'm impressed that you've got the requisite pot of gold at the end of it, too."

Lily smiled. "The pot of gold was Sam's idea," she said. It was actually a battered copper kettle the teenager had rescued from a trash bin, scrubbed up, and filled with foil-wrapped chocolate coins.

"Sam's idea, hmm? Somehow, having talked to him, I'm not surprised. He is one very savvy seventeen-year-old. A dedicated capitalist."

"His goal is to be a millionaire before his twenty-first birthday."

"So he said today. He'll probably make it."

"Paisley says she has the nightmare he'll end up being investigated by the Securities and Exchange Commission."

Dylan laughed, shifting closer to her. "I'd say that's within the realm of possibility, too."

Their thighs brushed. Lily dipped her chin, letting her hair swing forward. She found herself studying Dylan's long, lean legs. The rip in the left knee of his jeans seemed as endearing as it was incongruous.

Endearing. Lord, that was the last word she'd have picked to associate with Dylan Chase. But given the way he'd behaved today . . .

He'd showed her a facet of his personality she hadn't known existed. In doing so, he'd forced her to reevaluate her perceptions of him, to reexamine the conclusions she had so resentfully formed during their first meeting.

"I'm willing to bet the rainbow itself was your idea," Dylan commented after a few seconds.

Lily turned her head to look at him, her face still partially hidden by her tumble of hair. "It was my father's idea originally," she admitted. "When I was little—about five—he painted a rainbow on the wall of my bedroom in the house we were renting. I had to leave it behind, of course, when we moved. But I took the memory of all those colors with me. I never forgot what it felt like to have my own personal rainbow."

Dylan slipped his arm around her shoulders. "You were very close to your parents, weren't you?" he asked softly. While she still hadn't told him much about her background, she had confided a few details. He knew she'd been orphaned at age ten and sent to live with relatives in Boston. But that was about all he knew.

"Yes," she confirmed simply. "My parents were very

special people." She breathed in deeply, aware of the musky, sweat-tinged scent of him. She wondered about the taste of his perspiration . . . about the texture of his skin.

Dylan cleared her face of its curtain of hair with gentle fingers. The tawny tresses were soft. Her hair was thick but very fine and carried the faint fragrance of lemons and sunshine. He could visualize it spread out over one of the pillows on his bed. "You're the one who's special, Lily Bancroft," he murmured, tracing the delicate rim of her ear. "Very special . . . and very beautiful." Desire was throbbing deep in his vitals. Yet there was something else—something tentative and tender—stirring within him as well.

Lily shook her head slowly. His eyes had taken on the compelling topaz cast she had seen before. "No . . ." she denied.

"Yes."

"Dylan—"

"Lily . . . shh." And he bent his head to kiss her.

With seductive persuasiveness, he brushed his mouth against hers. Once. Twice. Three times. His caresses were lingering . . . leisurely. The taste of her was as sweet as he remembered it being.

Lily inhaled shakily as she felt Dylan languidly outline the contours of her lips with the tip of his tongue. She tilted her chin up in instinctive offering. One of his hands slid to the back of her head. The cup of his palm encouraged her yielding movement without commanding acquiescence.

Quivering, she made a throaty sound. She succumbed willingly to the sensations he was arousing. Quicksilver threads of excitement wove through her consciousness. Emotions awoke within her she hadn't known were sleeping . . . emotions she hadn't even known she was capable of feeling.

She stroked up the front of his chest, feeling the ripple of his muscles through the knit fabric of his shirt. His breathing altered in response to her tactile exploration. She pressed her palms flat against him, measuring the leaping increase in the pace of his heartbeat.

His lips settled hungrily over hers, his tongue searching . . . delving. She answered back with a tantalizing thrust of her own tongue. He made her feel as though her mouth was some succulent treat, a delicacy that had been created to be sampled and savored.

Coaxing . . . courting . . . he slowly penetrated the barriers the experiences of her formative years had made her construct. Dylan was a demanding, but not a selfish, lover. He had always found as much satisfaction in giving pleasure as in getting it.

Lily arched as his hands moved insinuatingly underneath her sweater and flowed up her rib cage to claim her breasts. She shifted restlessly, her body flowering in answer to his expertly erotic attentions. Tiny shivers skittered across the surface of her sensitive skin.

She was wearing a bra. Touch told Dylan it was a wispy bit of satin lace. The texture of it was pretty, even provocative, against his fingertips, and he took a few seconds to appreciate it. A few seconds, but no more.

"Mmm—" Lily was conscious of the deft movement of his fingers in the cleft between her breasts. She felt the clasp of her bra open. The delicate piece of lingerie was pushed aside.

Dylan had no intention of rushing her. But his confidence in his normally iron control wavered badly as the silken firmness of her naked breasts filled his hands. Desire, honed to razor-sharp urgency by a potent combination of denial and anticipation, sliced away at his ability to restrain himself.

"Can you feel how much I want you, Lily?" he asked hoarsely, scattering a searing trail of kisses up and down her throat. He feasted on her smooth flesh. Nipping. Nibbling. Nuzzling. "Can you feel what you do to me?"

Yes, she could feel it. Dylan had pressed her down against the sofa cushions by this time, one of his knees riding intimately between her thighs. Despite the denim constraint of his tight-fitting jeans, the assertive thrust of his arousal was obvious.

Perhaps it was the blatancy of his maleness that triggered her first flash of alarm at what was happening. Perhaps it was the sudden surge of domination in his caresses. . . .or the hot, honeyed sense of helplessness she felt threatening to overwhelm her. Lily never knew for certain. But something—*something*—touched off a tremor of panic within her.

"Dylan—"

He heard the protest, weak as it was. And he felt the beginnings of resistance in her body, too. He ignored both. Instead of pulling back, he sought and seized her lips again.

It was a sign of how far she had lowered her defenses, of how deeply in his thrall she was, that she nearly yielded to the branding, almost brutal, power of this new kiss. If Dylan had tempered the force of the claim he was imposing for just one second, if he'd allowed her a hint of a choice, she would have surrendered herself to him. But he didn't.

"Stop." She twisted, freeing her mouth. "Please—*no*."

How long did the silence that followed those three words last? A few moments? A whole minute? More?

However long it lasted, it was long enough for Dylan to fight a silent battle with himself. And long enough for him to come to a realization that shook him to the core.

Staring down at her, seeing her vulnerability, he knew he had the experience to change her no to a yes.

The look of dazed emotion in her eyes, the hectic flush of excitement in her cheeks, told him just how easy it would be. She was stiff and still against him now, fighting the bonds of attraction between them; but he could have her trembling and ready again . . .

He could have her, period.

But it wouldn't be enough.

Dylan made his decision and acted on it. He levered himself off Lily and moved to a sitting position. His posture was rigid, his breathing self-consciously steady. He closed his brain ruthlessly to the clamoring protests of his body. Frustration gnawed at him. So did the shamed knowledge of how very close he had come to forcing Lily.

The loss of Dylan's weight and warmth made Lily feel more bereft than anything else. She sat up, shakily, after several seconds and made a fumbling effort to restore some semblance of order to her clothing and hair. Her breasts ached with yearning. So did the secret places between her thighs. Her kiss-bruised mouth throbbed.

"Dylan—" she managed huskily, at last.

He had been staring straight ahead, his profile harsh and set. He turned his head at the sound of her voice. "I want you, Lily," he said without inflection. The colorless quality of his deep voice wasn't due to a lack of emotion—just the opposite, in fact.

"I . . . I know."

"And you want me." His amber-brown gaze was brilliant.

Lily looked down, unable to sustain his gaze. She was also unable to deny his flat assertion. "Dylan . . . I—it's too soon," she got out. She needed time, desperately. Time to sort out her feelings. Time to try to put things in perspective. Time to come to terms with the fact that she was deeply and inalterably drawn to a man who epitomized the world of wealth and position she'd turned her back on.

"Too soon? What have you got, Lily? Some kind of schedule for this sort of thing?"

Her head snapped up. "Do you?" she countered, stung. "Dylan, we met less than a week ago. We barely know each other."

"I know what I need to know."

She bridled at the arrogance and the autocratic certainty she heard in his words. "Well, I don't!" she retorted. What was worse, she didn't know *what* she needed to know anymore. The more she learned about Dylan Chase, the more mixed up she became.

Dylan's eyes narrowed. "You apparently knew enough a few minutes ago to nearly give in to me."

His choice of words made her heart clench. "Is that how you think of it? My 'giving in' to you?"

Dylan recognized instantly that he was losing her. He also recognized that the defenses she was retreating behind were very old and very entrenched. He reproached himself savagely not only for what he'd just said, but also for his earlier loss of self-control. "Lily—"

"That *is* what you're used to, isn't it? Having people defer . . . give in . . . say yes. It's so easy for you to be in charge—" She swallowed painfully. "You're so accustomed to being on top, Dylan. Did you ever think about what it does to the people *underneath?*"

There was a long silence. Lily watched as Dylan got up off the couch. She didn't regret the words she'd spoken. She'd had to say them.

Dylan was only vaguely conscious of having stood. Whatever else he was used to, he wasn't used to having this kind of challenge thrown at him. But it didn't anger him so much as it unsettled him. Then again, Lily Bancroft had done nothing but unsettle him since the moment he'd laid eyes on her.

He looked at her. The expression in his eyes shook the barriers she had slammed back into place. It made her want to reach out to him. But she didn't.

"Maybe, Lily. . ." Dylan said slowly, softly, almost more to himself than to her. "Maybe you know me better than you think." He offered her his hand and then he offered her his smile. It was a smile Lily had never seen before. "Didn't you say there was some cleaning up to do?" he asked.

She waited for a few moments, trying to assimilate what had happened. When the few moments were up, she nodded. Then she took his hand and matched his smile with one of her own.

Lily saw Dylan frequently during the next twelve days. It wasn't always easy to coordinate their schedules, but they managed. Geography—uptown versus downtown, the East Village versus the Upper East Side—caused a few problems, too, but nothing insurmountable.

Lily enjoyed their time together. Most of what they did was unplanned and spontaneous. Most of what they did was also either inexpensive or free, because she continued to insist on paying her own way.

She saw a surprising amount of Gary Chase, too, during the nearly two weeks following the scene in the loft. He popped up at the playhouse unexpectedly a number of times, claiming to be conducting an evaluation for the foundation. It was clear, however, he was indulging in an intense personal curiosity about Lily. She found herself putting up with him because, despite his obvious faults and sometimes clownish behavior, he was a genuinely likable person.

Just how Gary found out when her birthday was, Lily never learned. He refused to say, although he cheerfully admitted to passing the information on to his older brother. Dylan, in turn, calmly informed her he intended to take her out to dinner on the appropriate night. When she protested that she had to work, he told her everything had been arranged.

It certainly had been!

"Happy birthday, Lily," Dylan said, raising a Baccarat champagne flute to her. He was hawkishly handsome in a dark dinner jacket, perfectly at home in the sophisticated atmosphere of one of New York City's finest French restaurants.

"Thank you," she smiled, acknowledging his salute with a nod, then taking a sip of the sparkling wine. The delicate bubbles in it burst against her palate in tiny, icy explosions.

"Aren't you glad I bulldozed you into this?" he teased.

Lily laughed. "You had some help from Paisley. She told me it was illegal for her to allow me to work tonight."

"Oh, indeed. I understand it's a little-known provision in the bylaws of the Theater Guild."

"Actually, she said it would be a violation of my civil rights." She drank a little more champagne.

"That, too," he agreed. His vivid smile tempered into something softer as he studied her across the table. "You look very beautiful tonight," he told her. His eyes flowed over her, seeking and stirring responses.

"Thank you—again." She'd found the café-au-lait lace dress she had on in a tiny secondhand shop that specialized in stage costumes and theatrical props. With its seed-pearl beadwork and distinctly slinky cut, the garment had a vaguely twenties feel. Lily had purchased it on the spot. It had taken her months to find the perfect accessories. But the time—to say nothing of the money—had been well spent, because each time she dressed up in the outfit, she felt incredibly and uncharacteristically glamorous.

Of course, it would have been hard for her not to feel glamorous, given her companion and the setting he'd chosen. She glanced around the restaurant. The refined formality of the establishment's cream and gold decor created an aura that was opulent without being oppressive. There were masses of fresh flowers everywhere, and a number of exquisite watercolor pictures of gardens hung on the walls in gilt frames. No matter what season it was outside, it would always be spring in this lovely place.

Lilly spooned up some of the *soufflé glacé aux framboises*— cold raspberry soufflé—she'd ordered at the end of the meal. She savored the intensity of the dessert's bright-crimson raspberry sauce, smiling across at Dylan.

"Do you approve?" he asked, repeating the question she'd asked him over their first dinner together.

"Oh, yes," she assured him. She let her eyes rove around the room again. "You know," she observed thoughtfully, "I have the feeling this restaurant is to you what Guido's and Angelina's is to me."

"I do come here fairly often." He'd learned something new about her tonight. She spoke French. When she'd made her selections from the menu, her accent had been flawless. She also had more than a passing familiarity with wine lists, although she drank very sparingly. "But the owner hasn't gotten to the point where he throws his arms around me when I walk in."

"Too bad."

"On the other hand, the chef does let me order what I want." There was a wicked gleam in his eyes. "They offer some very intriguing *spécialités gourmandes* here."

"Mmm." Lily was beginning to feel pleasantly warm

and more than a little aroused. She had the distinct impression that the "gourmet specialty" Dylan Chase was intrigued by was Birthday Girl *du jour*. "I can imagine."

"Perhaps—" Dylan stopped abruptly, staring over her shoulder. It took him a second or so to accept that he was seeing what he was seeing. Once he did, he jumped—no, positively leaped—to the same conclusion he'd come to slightly more than three weeks before, when he'd been told that Snow White was waiting in the reception area.

"Dylan?" Lily asked, startled by the change in his expression. She was vaguely aware that the hushed hum of conversation in the restaurant had dropped to near silence.

"Do you remember telling me you think I may be too hard on my brother? That you think I should let him march to the beat of his own drummer, even if most of his marching seems to involve tripping over his own feet?"

Bewildered, Lily nodded. "I realize your styles are different. You favor suits, he goes for sneakers and sweatpants. You like organization. Your brother thrives on chaos." Lily sighed. "But Gary's been very helpful to us. He called a couple of days ago to say the foundation's board of trustees has our grant application under consideration."

"I know." He also knew that the decision to approve had already been made. While the playhouse had been endorsed for funding on its own merits, his personal intervention had speeded up the process significantly.

"But—"

"Do you also remember accusing me of exaggeration when I described some of his practical jokes?"

"Dylan, *what* is going on?"

"Turn around and see for yourself."

Lily did. What she saw was a very tall person in a very hairy black gorilla suit. In addition to the very hairy gorilla suit, the very tall person was wearing a top hat and tuxedo. He—she assumed it was a he—was heading toward their table with a determined but dignified stride.

"Oh . . . my . . . *God,"* she gasped, turning back to Dylan. "Dylan!"

"You can try hiding behind your napkin," he said. "But I don't think it will help."

The gorilla arrived. The restaurant had gotten so quiet, Lily thought she heard the bubbles in her champagne popping.

"Miss Lily Bancroft?" the gorilla inquired. His voice was beautifully resonant. Operatic, even.

Lily nodded mutely. She wasn't certain which she wanted to do more: sink under the table or burst into hysterical laughter. Maybe she'd try both.

The gorilla doffed his hat and bowed. Then he angled toward Dylan. "And you must be Mr. Dylan Chase, chief executive officer of ChaseCo International?"

"I must be," Dylan replied. He was going to kill his younger brother and plead temporary insanity afterward.

"Excellent." The gorilla bowed again. "I own a few shares of stock in your corporation. Keep up the good work."

"Oh, I will," Dylan returned dryly. He decided to forget the plea of temporary insanity. Murdering Gary because of this would definitely be justifiable homicide.

Lily made a choking sound as the gorilla turned back to her. "Ah—yes?" she wavered.

"I bring you singing birthday greetings from Mr. Garrison Chase." The gorilla seemed to grin.

"Singing?"

"Yes. If you would stand up, please, Miss Bancroft?"

"Do I have to?"

"Oh, absolutely."

Sighing, Lily stood.

- 5 -

"YOU REALIZE, OF course, we can never go back to that restaurant again," Dylan said, running his hand back through his thick, polished mahogany hair.

"Oh, I don't know," Lily returned, wrinkling her nose reflectively. "Considering the denomination of the bill I saw you slip the headwaiter as we were leaving, I think *you* still might be able to get a table there."

It was about an hour and a half later, and they were sitting in Lily's loft, drinking champagne. Dylan had discarded his jacket, pulled his tie loose, and undone the top two buttons of his dress shirt. Lily had kicked off her strappy high-heeled sandals. Her fashionably upswept hair was no longer pristinely swept up. Tendrils of it curled about her temples and down her neck. She toyed absently with several strands as she gazed at Dylan.

His well-defined mouth twisted ruefully at her observation. "I suppose I should be thankful Gary didn't alert the media," he commented wryly.

"The Lone Wolf of Wall Street Meets a Manhattan Monkey," Lily said, conjuring a possible headline.

"Snow White Meets King Kong," he countered. He shook his head. "Actually, I'm surprised my brother wasn't lurking around under one of the other tables so he could witness the fun for himself."

"Maybe he decided discretion was the better part of valor in this instance," Lily commented delicately.

"If you're suggesting I might have gone after Gary with a blunt instrument, you're probably right."

"Chase Chases Chase."

He gave a brief chuckle. He had been angry, yes. But once the initial shock had worn off, and he'd been certain that Lily hadn't been offended by being placed in such an embarrassing situation, he'd begun to see the humor in the episode. "Something like that."

Lily smiled. His hair was almost as disheveled as it had been the day of the softball game. She wanted to muss it up even more. "Well, at least the gorilla had a wonderful voice," she noted. "I don't think I've ever heard such a good a cappella version of 'Happy Birthday to You.' Everyone in the restaurant applauded."

Dylan lifted his glass of champagne. "Trust my brother to locate the Luciano Pavarotti of primates." He started to laugh suddenly. "Oh, God. *Gary.*"

Lily laughed, too. She laughed until she ran out of breath, nearly splashing herself with champagne in the process. "It's all right, then?" she asked, leaning forward on the sofa to set her glass on the rattan chest in front of it. Straightening, she gazed questioningly at Dylan, putting her right hand lightly on his upper arm. The silk of his shirt was very fine and she could feel the smooth, muscled warmth of his bicep through it.

His laughter stopped and his intense eyes gleamed

with flecks of gold as they met hers. "Yes," he told her. "It's all right."

She made a small movement to withdraw her hand, but he covered it with his own. His touch was firm yet gentle. Lily felt it clear down to her curling, stockinged toes. "I—I like to hear you laugh," she said. The sound of his laughter, unforced and rich, delighted her. "You don't do it often enough."

His brows went up. "Are you saying I don't have a good sense of humor?"

"No," she denied quickly. "You have a wonderful sense of humor—even if you *do* think Road Runner cartoons are better than Tweety Bird's." She was sincere. He had a wry wit that appealed to her tremendously. He didn't reduce her to a pile of helpless giggles the way Howie often had during their marriage, but he did tickle her funny bone—and her brain.

"I'm glad you approve." He stroked the hand he had possession of, tracing the slender fingers from knuckle to nail. "I like to hear you laugh, too." He lifted her hand to his mouth and kissed the back of it, never letting his eyes leave hers. Watching. Waiting. Willing her to want him as much as he wanted her.

The air in the loft had seemed cool and still to Lily when she and Dylan had come in. Now it felt sultry and stirring, as though a storm were building inside the space. Lily liked storms. She always had. She liked the fierce freedom, the unchallengeable power of them. One of the few memories of unalloyed happiness she had from her childhood years with her Aunt Amanda had to do with the August afternoon she'd stood on a Cape Cod beach, face tilted, eyes closed, arms lifted, welcoming the wild summer storm that had been sweeping in from the sea.

"What . . . else do you like to hear, Dylan?" she asked softly. Her mouth curved as she saw the gold in his eyes blaze to life then melt.

"I like to hear you say my name," he answered.

She brought her free hand up and carefully brushed back the brown-red shock of hair that had fallen down onto his forehead. "How do you like to hear me say it?"

"Any way. Every way."

She gave him a taste of her lips then, enjoying the champagne-tinged flavor of his as she did. He took what she offered hungrily, but controlled the greed for more that erupted within him as soon as their mouths merged.

"Mmm . . . Dylan," she half-murmured, half-sighed, when the kiss ended.

"That's one way." She was like a festival for the senses. Fresh. Fragrant. Female. He celebrated her with his eyes and hands.

"Dylan-n-n," Lily stretched the second syllable, stroking it as though it was something she could actually touch. In a way she couldn't explain, even to herself, saying his name over and over seemed a fitting prelude to the possession she now knew she wanted. "And that's another way."

This time, he began the kiss. Began it, deepened it, prolonged it. He nipped at her lower lip as though he intended to devour it bit by tiny, tender bit, then sucked the whole of it into his mouth.

This time, when their mouths parted, he was the one who spoke. He said her name huskily. Her face flowered into a smile, telling him how much she relished what she heard.

Lily let her fingers drift up his shirtfront, ticking off each small button. She lingered for a few seconds at the apex of the triangle of bare skin at the base of his throat, then reversed direction.

One button. Two. Three . . .

Desire sprinted through him like an Olympic runner as she opened his shirt. He caught his breath convulsively as she caressed his naked chest for the first time.

Happy birthday to me, Lily thought with a dizzying sense of power as she registered his reactions. She rubbed her hands over his chest, touching everywhere. She had to learn each variation in the textures of him, from the smoothness of his skin, to the crisp spring of his chest hair, to the furled hardness of his male nipples. Her tactile curiosity coated his sleekly muscled torso like hot oil.

Dylan covered her mouth, absorbing the breath she would have used to evoke his name yet again. He shifted her body against him. Slender. Soft. Supple.

One of his hands tangled in her hair, demolishing what was left of her seductive, sophisticated upsweep. The other moved to the nape of her neck, searching for the tab of her zipper. The promise of her skin had beckoned to him all during dinner through the intricate patterning of her lace dress. He needed that promise fulfilled.

There was no zipper. There were buttons. Dozens of them.

Dylan groaned inwardly, then gave a brief prayer of gratitude that he had made the discovery now, while he still had the patience to at least try to undo them. He knew himself well enough to realize that a few minutes more exposure to the taste and touch of Lily Bancroft would render him incapable of doing anything but ripping the back of her dress open.

Yes, oh yes, Lily thought urgently as she felt Dylan's fingers begin to work their way down her spine. She was only dimly conscious of the kind of obstacle course her garment must be presenting. The fit of her dress eased then loosened then went completely slack.

"Not on the sofa," Dylan rasped out. The meaning of his words swam through the simmering fluidity of Lily's thoughts. She nodded her agreement.

Lily's queen-sized, quilt-covered bed was in the far corner, separated from the rest of the loft by rice paper screens. Much, much later, she discovered that the route she and Dylan took to reach it was anything but direct. Their wildly meandering path was marked by the clothes they'd stripped off and scattered at they went.

Hunger. Heat. *Him.* Lily tumbled back against the mattress of her bed, bringing Dylan down with her. She craved the contrast of him, the way his masculinity complemented and enhanced her femininity. Hard. Soft. Rough. Smooth. Strong. Delicate.

Dylan cupped her breasts, cajoling the fair-skinned globes to straining peaks, coaxing the rosy tips into quivering buds. Bending his head, he took one of her nipples deep into his mouth, suckling at it until Lily cried out. He kissed his way to her other breast then, and claimed it, too.

The frantic desire to touch, to know, to claim, that had been born within her when she'd tugged back his shirt had grown into a wildness that was raging through her. It burned through her bloodstream. It seared into every cell of her brain. It was a fever that demanded to be fed and fed and fed again. It could not be satisfied, only stoked higher and hotter.

Her hands roamed over him. There were no boundaries to restrain her, no barriers to stop her. His skin was sheened with perspiration now. Her tongue absorbed its salty tang even as her fingers admired its slickness. She felt his lean muscles tense then ease, grow rigid then relax, in answer to her explorations.

Dylan had wanted before, but not with this kind of unreasoning, unmanageable force. He had needed before, but never to the point of a pain so urgent, so elemental, it could not go unrelieved.

"Lily—" His voice was thick in his throat. He could

have shown her his want, his need, but something compelled him to speak the words. "Love, please—"

Lily didn't give in. She simply gave. Dylan filled her, hot and hard. He drove himself, he drove her. She met him, matched him, and marveled at every rapturous moment of it.

Blinded. Breathless. There was a split second of complete stillness and total silence betwen them. Then the stillness and silence exploded, as they did, into something too powerful, too overwhelming, to be denied. It was utterly, endlessly shattering. And it was too much to be sustained alone or unchanged.

"Dylan?" Lily said suddenly, out of an obscure, bliss-hazed reverie. She was lying with her cheek resting against his chest, listening to his heartbeat.

"Mmm?" Dylan responded, straining the tawny silk of her hair through his fingers. Sanity, of a kind, had returned sometime before, and he'd used what little unspent strength he had to shift his weight off her. He'd settled her in the cradle of his right arm and shoulder. She'd curled up, like a kitten seeking warmth, her pliant body melting effortlessly into an intimate fit with his. He'd felt her slender fingers feather along his skin as she'd made her murmuring movements of adjustment. Astoundingly, he'd experienced the first stirrings of renewed desire at her touch.

Lily lifted her head. She hadn't turned on the lights in this part of the loft when they'd come in, but there was enough illumination spilling in from the living room area to allow her to make out the details of his face. He looked relaxed, even sleepy. His long-lashed eyelids were drooping a bit, as though he was too lazy to keep them fully open. There was a distinctly satisfied set to the line of his mouth.

Lily discovered an intense pride in the knowledge

that she was the one who had given Dylan this palpable aura of deeply sensuous contentment.

She felt sated but not at all sleepy. Not even drowsy. No, her body was pleasantly charged up, and seemed enveloped in the tingling afterglow of their passionate lovemaking.

"Lily?" Dylan prompted, his velvety voice liquifying what little solidity her bones had regained.

She blinked. "I was wondering about Rodgers."

"Rodgers?" he repeated blankly. Why in heaven's name would she—? Dylan was well aware that Lily's mind occasionally worked in very mysterious ways; but, for the life of him, he couldn't begin to imagine what had sent her thoughts heading off in this unlikely direction. "Rodgers, my driver?"

Lily nodded, her curtain of hair bouncing with the up-down movement. "You left him out in the car when we came back here from the restaurant."

"You—ah—think I should have invited him in?" he hazarded a guess, letting the palm of one hand glide slowly up her back. The shadowy dimness lent a bewitching delicacy to her face. He wondered if she had any idea how her eyes were shining.

Lily made a small sound of irritation. "Don't be obtuse," she chided.

He chuckled softly. "Sweetheart," he told her with husky honesty, "I don't think I have the energy to be obtuse."

She nibbled at her lower lip. The kiss-bruised flesh was very tender. So were several other parts of her body. "Are you—are you going to stay here all night?" she asked at last.

Dylan's energy level went up perceptibly in response to this question. "If you'll let me," he told her quietly, a hint of topaz smoke spiraling in his eyes. "I want to be with you, Lily. I want to fall asleep with you in my arms and I want to wake up the same way."

A hot, sweet thrill sped through Lily at his words. But she forced herself to concentrate on the subject she'd initially raised, despite the fact that she was having serious trouble remembering *why* she'd raised it. "I—what about Rodgers? He's sitting out there . . . where it's cold . . ."

"While we're lying in here . . . where it's warm . . ."

"Y-yes."

His teeth gleamed white. "Is it Rodgers you're worried about, or your reputation?" he asked teasingly.

"Dylan—" She felt herself flush. The truthful answer to his question was both, although she wanted to believe that the chauffeur's welfare was her first concern. She did *not* want to think that her anxiety about her "reputation"—or, at least, about what Rodgers might think of her—was in any way connected to her Aunt Amanda's repeated lectures on the necessity of behaving discreetly in front of servants.

"It's all right," he said easily. "Unless I miss my guess, Rodgers is snug in his own apartment by this time, probably enjoying a nightcap with his wife."

"But how—"

"Before we came by to pick you up, I told him that once we got back from the restaurant, he should wait a half an hour and then leave. With or without me."

This flat statement triggered off a barrage of contradictory emotions in Lily. She looked down at his chest, her eyes studying the curly mat of reddish-brown hair there. "You were—" she stopped, swallowing. "You were very sure about me tonight, weren't you, Dylan?"

He hooked her chin up with two fingers. "No, I wasn't," he returned concisely. Uncertainty. It was a difficult thing for him to admit to. But he'd admit to it where Lily Bancroft was concerned. "If I had been, I wouldn't have told Rodgers to wait thirty seconds, much less thirty minutes."

An edge of anger. An unconscious arrogance. And an absolute honesty. Lily could hear all of them in his unvarnished assertion. She could hear them, but she didn't know what to say in answer.

"Lily—" Dylan hesitated, choosing his words carefully because they mattered so much. "I'm not 'very sure' about you. I don't think I've ever been *less* sure about a woman in my life." He moved his hand, tangling it deep in her hair. "There are moments when I feel closer to you than I've ever felt to anyone. But there are other moments—*lots* of other moments—when I feel I don't know you at all."

The gleaming amber fragments in his dark eyes had turned to tiny flames, licking at the brown of his irises. The intensity of his gaze made Lily tremble, but she didn't turn away from it. "Two weeks ago, you said you knew what you needed to know," she remined him.

"I was wrong."

She kept staring at him. "When I first met you, I thought I could be very sure about you," she confessed slowly. "I thought I knew what *I* needed to know. But I was wrong, too. I—I'm not any surer than you are, right now."

There was a silence between them then. Dylan let it lengthen, stretch taut, and finally break against the audible change in their breathing patterns. He drew her up until her face was level with his. He held her that way for a few seconds, her feminine softness pressing against him, his male hardness thrusting against her.

"There is one thing I'm sure about," he whispered.

He claimed her then, without hesitation. And Lily was sure as well.

* * *

Normally, Lily surfaced out of a night's sleep quickly and cleanly, coming awake almost instantly. This morning, however, the process was a deliciously gradual one. The transition from complete oblivion to a sort of dream state was pleasurably slow. She lingered there until the seductive drift of Dylan's fingers wooed her to full awareness.

She turned over with a sensuous movement that was half-roll, half-stretch. Her eyelids seemed incredibly heavy for a moment, then floated open as though helium balloons had been attached to her long, light-brown lashes.

Lily examined her lover of a single night tranquilly. He was propped up on one elbow, studying her. "Good morning," she said with a smile.

"Good morning," he returned, smoothing her hair back from her cheeks and forehead. He'd buried his face in her hair the night before, after the second time he'd found his release. He'd been gasping, unable to control his breathing or the tremors shaking his body. The toffee-colored strands had been like vibrant threads of raw silk against his skin.

Lily filled her lungs with a long, deep breath, reveling in her sense of well-being. "I feel like a celebration," she announced.

Dylan grinned. "Another one? I think you've had your celebration, Lily. Several of them, in fact."

The gleam in his eyes as he said this made Lily color even as she laughed. The sound of her laughter was as languid as the back-forth shake of her head. "No, no," she corrected. "'I feel like a celebration' as in *being* one. Not, 'I feel like a celebration' as in having one! Although, since you've brought the subject up . . ." She let her voice trail off on an insinuating note. At the same time, she trailed her right hand down Dylan's hair-roughened chest. Her fingers looked very pale against his tanned skin.

Dylan trapped her roving hand about two inches from the point where the invitation in its descent would have become impossible to refuse. He carried the hand to his lips and turned it over, kissing the center of her palm. "Do you know what time it is?" he inquired, releasing her. As was his habit, he'd awoken early and instantly alert. But for once, he hadn't been gripped by the automatic compulsion to confront the day. Instead, he'd been content to lie beside Lily, watching her sleep.

"Umm . . ." she glanced upward. There was a skylight overhead. It was the main reason she'd chosen to put her bed in this corner of the loft. She might not stand outside in storms anymore, but still liked communing with the weather. "It's sometime . . . mmm . . . Saturday. Morning."

Dylan chuckled at her vagueness. "It's past eight-thirty."

Lily blinked, conscious of a tiny flutter of alarm. "Do you—do you have somewhere to go?" she asked, keeping her voice light. She'd thought . . . assumed . . .

Dylan saw the flicker of disquiet in her eyes. "I'm not going anywhere, Lily," he said. Seven-day work weeks might be the usual order of business for the Lone Wolf of Wall Street, but not this weekend. Dylan was exactly where he wanted to be. "But you've got a matinee today, remember?"

She relaxed. "That's not for hours."

"What about that Saturday-morning workshop you were telling me about last night? The one for the fourteen overactive fourth-graders."

"The Dirty Dozen and the Kamikaze Twins aren't

due until ten-thirty," she replied airily. "And everything's all set for them. We're doing hand jive this week."

"Hand jive?"

"That's what they call puppetry." She laughed. "It's also known as thumb theater."

"I see." He slipped one of his hands beneath the large, brightly colored quilt that covered their bodies.

"Do you want to sit in?" Lily asked impulsively, then hesitated, not certain how he'd react to the idea. "Sam Stevens sometimes works with me," she explained after a second. "But he's taking his College Board tests today. I could use an ext—*ah!*" She broke off suddenly, her eyes widening as his warm palm molded the curve of her hip.

"Yes?" Dylan prompted blandly. The smile that touched his mouth was distinctly male. "You were saying you could use—?"

"I—" She swallowed. She'd been going to say that she could use an extra hand. Somehow, that particular phrase seemed a bit too provocative at this moment. "I could use some extra help," she substituted.

"Mmm." Dylan didn't have to speculate anymore on how sexual arousal affected Lily's eye color. The green in her irises was bright and getting brighter. "Kids and puppets. I haven't had any experience in that area, I'm afraid. Just what kind of extra help could you use?"

"I-ohhh—" She sucked in her breath as she felt the tantalizing rake of his nails across her stomach. He circled the indentation of her navel with exquisitely erotic precision.

"Actually, it's not the dealing with the kids I'm concerned about," he went on meditatively, shifting himself until they were lying face to face. "It's the puppetry."

"The puppetry?" She arched against the intimate stroke of his fingers, excitement zigzagging through her like lightning.

"Mmm. I'm not sure I have the manual dexterity for it."

Lily arched again. "You're n-not?" she got out in a tone of disbelief. Was the man *crazy?*

"Nope." He coaxed her onto her back, shifting his body again. She felt the seeking nudge of his knee between her thighs. "And I wouldn't want to disappoint you, Lily."

Lily reached up, grasping his strong shoulders, "I—ah, *Dylan!* I—I wouldn't worry if I were you. You're very good with your han—mmm . . ."

He was very good with his lips, too.

Lily and Dylan were finishing up a hasty breakfast—fresh-squeezed grapefruit juice and whole wheat and raisin muffins—when the phone rang. It was shortly after ten.

Lily answered. "Gomph mmphng." Her greeting came out garbled. She cleared her throat of a half-swallowed bite of muffin and smiled over at Dylan. He smiled back. The voltage in the expression started low but built to the point where Lily expected her ponytailed hair to start crackling with static electricity.

He was wearing the dark trousers and the white silk dress shirt from the night before. The shirt was wrinkled and only partially buttoned. His hair was thoroughly disheveled and slightly damp from the shower they had shared before breakfast. There was a shadowing of stubble on his lean cheeks. To Lily, he looked faintly disreputable, unmistakably dangerous, and devastatingly sexy.

"Hel-lo?" the person on the other end of the line prompted.

"Um—good morning," Lily repeated, breaking eye contact with Dylan. Her diction was precise this time, but her voice wasn't entirely steady.

"Good morning. And how's the gorilla of my dreams?"

"The gor—" Lily nearly dropped the phone. *"Gary?"*

Dylan drained his glass and set it down very carefully. *Damn,* he thought with a mixture of frustration and foreboding. *Who's done what now?* The last time Gary had called him at a woman's apartment, it had been because he'd run out of money while hitchhiking to California, and was about to be run in for vagrancy by some small-town sheriff.

"Yeah, it's Gary. Don't hang up!"

Lily glanced at Dylan. He was watching her, his face unreadable. "What—what happens if I hang up?" she asked.

"I call back." The reply came very quickly. "Ah—about last night. You're not—ah—you know—"

Lily didn't say anything. No, she wasn't angry about last night's gorilla gag, which was obviously what he wanted to know. She had too strong a sense of humor not to relish the absurdity of the situation Gary had created. On the other hand, she didn't want to let him off the hook until he'd wiggled . . . just a little.

"Lily?"

She relented. "No, I'm not 'you know.' But that's not to say I'm not going to find out when *your* birthday is."

Dylan's younger brother chuckled, plainly relieved. "Phew. You had me going there for a minute. So you believe in the motto 'Don't get mad, get even,' hmm?

Well, that's just another thing you and Dylan have in common." This casually made assertion was followed by a brief pause. Something in the quality of the silence coming from the other end of the line made Lily stiffen.

"Gary—" she began.

"Look, Lily, if he's there, I need to talk to him."

Green-gray eyes homed in and locked on amber-brown ones. Dylan rose from his seat in a lithe movement, walked noiselessly over to where she was standing, and took the phone. Lily took a step away from him.

Dylan put the receiver to his ear. "I hope, for your sake, that you've got a good reason for calling, Gary," he said pleasantly. Too pleasantly, Lily decided. The change in him was decidedly unnerving.

"Aren't you going to ask how I knew what restaurant to send the gorilla to?"

Dylan took a deep breath. "Since you've repeatedly told me how predictable I am, I doubt it was any great feat of detective work. Now, *what's happened?"*

Lily clenched her fists. She'd heard that coolly implacable tone of command before. Too many times before. It was only used by people who'd become so accustomed to being obeyed, they scarcely considered the possibility of noncompliance.

"Diana showed up at mother's last night just as mother and eleven of her nearest and dearest friends-of-the-week were sitting down to dinner," Gary said flatly.

Dylan swore once, very quietly.

"Oh, but wait. There's more," his younger brother cautioned sardonically.

"There always is. Let me guess. She walked out on Arnold again and came crying home to mother."

"Right in one. Actually, Di's a lot more predictable than you are, Dyl."

"Gary—"

"Anyway. She was with Kerri. In hysterics."

"*Kerri* was in hysterics?"

"No, Diana. But Kerri wasn't in very good shape, either. They flew up from D.C. and the poor kid got air sick. She threw up all over the Oriental rug in the dining room."

"And then what happened?"

"And then *mother* got hysterical—I swear, it's hereditary—and did what all of us do when there's a crisis. She called you."

Dylan forked his hand back through his hair. He knew Lily was staring at him. She was staring at him, but he had the strangest sensation she was seeing someone else. "She called me and I wasn't there," he said, prodding Gary to go on.

"No, you weren't. So, she called the switchboard at ChaseCo and they didn't know where you were."

There were several seconds of silence. Dylan, for one of the very, very few times in his adult life, had not told the company switchboard how he could be reached in case of emergency. He supposed he should be feeling some kind of guilt. Instead, he was experiencing a wave of anger against his mother and sister. "So?" he questioned without inflection.

"So, mother got incredibly desperate and called me."

The silence this time was much longer than the previous one.

"Thanks, Gary," Dylan said very quietly. "I owe you one."

"No, you don't. Look, I'm sorry if I interrupted anything. I just figured you should know what's waiting for you uptown." Gary laughed carelessly. "Take my advice, stay down in the East Village. Bye, Dylan."

"I'll talk to you later, Gary," Dylan responded, and

broke the connection. He reached out for Lily and pulled her against his chest.

She let herself be drawn to him. "A family problem?" she asked, feeling his mouth brush briefly over her temple.

He gave an ironic laugh, his breath fanning her skin. "A problem family," he amended.

She tilted her face so she could look at him. The rakish, tender lover was gone. "Something to do with your niece, Kerri?" she probed. Although Dylan's end of the conversation had been terse, she'd been able to pick up that much detail.

"Kerri's mother. Diana's third marriage is apparently going down for the third time."

"And you've got to play lifeguard?"

His mouth twisted. "God, no. I told her from the beginning Arnold wasn't a suitable husband."

"Oh." Lily suddenly felt very fragile.

Dylan traced the outline of her lips with one finger. "Can I get a raincheck on the hand jive workshop?"

She nodded. "Of course . . . anytime."

He drew her gently into his arms. "I have to go, really. I hope you'll understand."

Lily melted against him, trying to suppress a sudden sense of sadness.

"Lily?"

"I understand," she told him. What she failed to add was that she wished she didn't.

- 6 -

"A-A-N-ND CUE CURTAIN," Paisley commanded softly, acting in her performance capacity as the Potluck Playhouse's stage manager. She tapped Lily lightly on the shoulder.

Lily—who had been shanghaied into working as low man on the stage crew totem pole for this particular Sunday matinee—responded by giving the curtain rope a smooth jerk. Pulling hand over hand, she opened the curtain to the point where the cast of *Hansel and Gretel Go Hollywood* could step forward and take their final bows.

Dylan and his young niece, Kerri, were out in the audience, she knew. She hoped they'd enjoyed the show. Although she'd spoken with him twice by phone in the past twenty-four hours, she hadn't seen Dylan since he'd left her loft the morning before to sort out his sister's marital problems. Lily was as anxious as a teenager about being with him again.

"A-a-n-n-d close curtain," Paisley ordered, heaving an audible sigh of relief. "Nice job, Lily."

Lily nodded, tugging on the coarse hemp cord once again. She winced absently as she heard the squeaks and groans of the winch and pulley system. Someday, she thought, we're going to get an electric curtain puller. *Someday*. . .

And someday, they were going to replace the lighting board, paint the lobby, and reupholster the seats, too.

The cast trooped off the stage, into the wings. They exchanged brief but predictable comments with Lily as they brushed by.

"Hi, Dave."

"Hi, Lil. Lookin' good, babe."

"Nice show, Suze."

"Yeah, I thought so. See you Tuesday."

"How's it going, Tom?"

"If that bitch Gretel steps on my lines one more time, I'm going to scratch her beady little eyes out!"

"Hi, Max. Good performance." Lily delivered this last greeting with genuine warmth. It was directed at Max Stendahl, the actor who played the handsome Hollywood stunt man who—in the playhouse's version of the old classic—saved Hansel and Gretel from the clutches of an evil gossip columnist. Max had appeared in several Potluck productions. Lily was friends with him and his wife, Zoe.

"Thanks, Lily," Max grinned. "You were pretty good yourself today, running the lights. It was nice to have the follow spot following me instead of the other way around. Any chance Zach's flu might be a permanent condition?" He winked.

Lily shook her head, smiling. "Sorry. He's just about recovered."

"Well, you can't win 'em all. Take care. Call Zoe. She wants to have lunch."

"I will. Bye, Max."

Max was succeeded by Joelle Peters, the veteran actress who played the evil gossip columnist. The older woman had just yanked off the carrot-colored wig she wore for her part. She was vigorously scratching her scalp.

"Hi, Joelle," Lily said cautiously. Joelle had thrown a snit during intermission, and Lily was wary of her mood.

Joelle plainly picked up on her uneasiness. "Oh, Lily, sweetie, I want to apologize for freaking out the way I did. I mean, so there was a mouse in my dressing room—you'd think that after more than twenty years in this business, I'd be used to dealing with rodents, right?"

Lily smiled in relief. "I understand," she said. "And I'm sorry, too. I've had the exterminators in three times in the last six weeks, I thought everything was taken care of."

"I know. I know."

"I'll call them again tomorrow."

"Thanks, honey." After patting Lily on the arm, Joelle strolled off, her well-padded hips swaying.

It was about ten minutes later when Dylan came backstage with his niece. Lily sensed his presence before she heard or spotted him. She simply felt the touch of his eyes, turned around, and he was there.

He kissed her briefly on the cheek, his hands lingering a bit longer on her waist. She smiled at him, her heart leaping.

"Lily, this is my niece, Kerri Phillips," he said after a moment. "Kerri, this is Miss Bancroft."

"Hello, Kerri." Lily bent slightly, extending her hand. "I'm pleased to meet you." The little girl's pale, pretty face had the sweet solemnity of a Victorian Alice in Wonderland. Her outfit—a navy pleated skirt and a matching Fair Isle sweater—reminded Lily of the uniform she had to wear at the private elementary school she'd been enrolled in by her Aunt Amanda.

"Hello, Miss Bancroft. I'm pleased to meet you, too," the child returned, shaking her hand politely. Then, happily, her grave shyness dissolved into a smile. "Your play was really neat! Especially the lady with the red hair."

"I'm glad you enjoyed yourself," Lily said sincerely.

"Uncle Dylan did, too. But I like plays. I was in one last year in school," Kerri volunteered proudly.

"Were you?"

"Uh-huh. I was the first robin of spring. I got to bow *four* times at the end when everybody was clapping."

"You must have been terrific, then," Lily said. "Are you thinking about being an actress when you grow up?"

Dylan's niece nodded emphatically, her long brown hair bouncing. "Or a ballerina. I took dance lessons this summer in Washington. I was going to take them again, only I don't think I can because if Mummy gets divorced from Arnold like she says she's going to do, we won't live there anymore." She paused, her brown eyes serious. "Arnold is Mummy's husband. He's a lawyer with the government. But he's not my real daddy. My *real* daddy lives in California," she clarified for Lily's benefit.

Lily glanced at Dylan, wondering how he was reacting to this outpouring of personal information. Unexpectedly, she saw a look of warmth in his eyes, as though Kerri's opening up to her pleased him. "I see, Kerri," she told the child gently.

"They have ballet lessons in New York, don't they? Maybe once Uncle Dylan tells Mummy what to do we can live here and I can take some." She gave Lily an innocent, confiding smile. "See, Uncle Dylan always knows what to do when Mummy's in trouble."

"He sounds like a very useful person to have around," Lily replied after a second.

"Oh, yes. Grandmama says she doesn't know what she'd do without him."

"Kerri—" Dylan said, deciding it was time he reined in his young niece's runaway tongue.

"Dylan!" This exclamation of greeting came from Paisley Stevens, who materialized beside them wearing a beaming smile. "I didn't realize you were going to be here today."

"Hello, Paisley," Dylan replied smoothly. He'd long since recognized the redhead as a potential ally and a possible key to understanding Lily's complicated nature. "It's good to see you again. I'd like to introduce my nice, Kerri. Kerri, this is Mrs. Stevens. Her son was the young man we talked to during intermission."

"Oh, he was nice!" Kerri exclaimed.

Sam's mother laughed. "I think so, too." She glanced back and forth between Lily and Dylan. Lily could practically hear the wheels turning beneath the untidy cap of titian curls. "You know, Kerri," Paisley remarked thoughtfully. "You look like the type of person who'd appreciate a special backstage tour of the Potluck Playhouse."

The suggestion was an instant hit. The little girl's face lit up like a Broadway marquee. She turned to Dylan. "Oh, can I?" she implored.

"If it's not too much trouble—" Dylan lifted his brows.

"No trouble at all," Paisley assured him blithely. "Come on, Kerri. Let's start with the dressing rooms."

"You know, the more I see of Paisley, the more I like her," Dylan grinned after his niece was escorted out of earshot.

"She has that effect on people," Lily conceded with a

laugh. She picked a bit of lint from her sleeve. Knowing she'd be seeing Dylan had prompted her to upgrade her usual workday outfit, and she'd traded her customary jeans and sweatshirt for a jade wool sweater and a pair of matching corduroy slacks. "I'm sorry I couldn't come out to see you during intermission."

"Sam explained you had to fill in for someone," he answered, stroking one finger lightly down her cheek. He wanted to touch her much more intimately, but he was hesitant about starting something he knew he wouldn't be able to finish.

"Actually, I was trying to deal with a backstage crisis," Lily replied. The look in his eyes triggered the same fluttering excitement inside her she felt on opening nights.

"The plumbing in the prop room?" he guessed.

"A mouse in one of the dressing rooms."

"Ah. I *thought* I heard the faint sounds of screaming earlier."

"Faint?" Lily scoffed. "Joelle Peters—the screamer—has a three-octave range and has been known to register on the Richter scale."

"I stand corrected." His voice dropped and darkened. "I also stand here having missed you like hell last night. I wanted to come back, but there was no way to get free."

"I understand," Lily told him softly, putting a hand on his arm. He was casually dressed, as he had been the night at the Village Gate, in gray twill slacks, a cashmere pullover, and a bombadier-style jacket of supple black leather. "I . . . what are you going to tell Diana to do?"

"Not, unfortunately, what I'd like to," he replied, grimacing. He shook his head. "I think I mentioned I was the one who told her she shouldn't marry Arnold."

Lily nodded slowly. "Maybe . . ." she hesitated, then

had to speak. "Maybe that's why she married him," she suggested. She knew she was drawing on her memories of how she'd reacted to being told what she should and shouldn't do.

Dylan's jaw tightened. What she was implying wasn't a completely new idea to him. "Maybe," he conceded, forcing himself to relax. He brushed Lily's cheek again. "I promised Kerri I'd take her to dinner after the play. Would you join us?"

Lily let the subject of Diana drop. It really wasn't her business, in any case. "I'd like that," she told him.

"I should warn you that I also promised her she could pick the place."

She slanted him a teasing look. "Careful, Mr. Chase, that could become a habit with you."

"I'll risk it. Afterward, we can drop her off at my mother's and—ah—" He cocked a brow.

"Afterward, I'll let *you* pick the place," Lily said demurely.

"Is Dylan coming by here tonight?" Paisley asked offhandedly a little over a week later. She gazed at Lily over the rim of her wineglass.

Lily suppressed a sigh, wondering how long her friend had been practicing her look of casual inquiry. It was almost as convincing as the casual way she'd invited herself up to the loft after this evening's performance. "I'm not sure," Lily answered. "It depends on how late the reception runs. He's got an early plane to Washington tomorrow."

"Hmm. That's the reception for the governor?"

Lily took a sip of her wine. "Yes, Paisley." As if you didn't know, Paisley, she added silently. She'd seen this conversation coming for some time. A part of her dreaded it. Another part of her desperately wanted to talk to someone.

"Are you sorry now you told Dylan you wouldn't go with him?"

"I had to work tonight, remember?" Lily swirled her wine around, her eyes fixed on the Chardonnay whirlpool she was creating in the bottom of her glass.

"You would have told him no even if you hadn't had to work," Paisley asserted flatly.

Lily didn't deny it. She couldn't. It was the truth. "What do you want me to say, Paisley? I didn't want to go tonight, all right? I didn't . . . I don't feel comfortable in that sort of situation. I don't fit in."

Paisley, who had been exhibiting an uncharacteristic degree of restraint, suddenly reverted to type. She snorted rudely. "If you ask me, Lily Wilding Bancroft, the reason you didn't want to go tonight is because you *do* feel comfortable in that sort of situation. Because you *do* fit in—whether you want to admit it or not."

Lily brought her head up with a jerk. She felt a bit like a piece of shish kebab meat—skewered right through the middle. "Paisley—" she began painfully.

"Lily, why don't you just tell Dylan about your background?"

"Because it's none of his business!"

"Are you afraid of how he might react?"

"No. Of course not!" Lily wished she didn't sound so defensive. She also wished she was surer of what she was saying. She put down her wineglass. "Look, my 'background,' as you call it, is just that. Background. History. *Past* history. It doesn't have anything to do with now . . . with me."

"You can't just chop ten years out of your life and pretend they never happened."

"I was doing a pretty good job of it until recently." Lily slumped against the sofa cushions. "Until I met Dylan Chase." She puffed up her cheeks with air, then exhaled it disgustedly. "*Snow White Versus the Lone*

Wolf of Wall Street, indeed," she muttered.

"Lily—"

"He's got me so confused!" she burst out. She'd been in a muddle from the moment she'd laid eyes on him—her body filled with a constant yearning, her brain fuzzed with unsettling thoughts. "Dylan is so—so—"

"Gorgeous? Smart? Sexy?" Paisley suggested instantly, reeling off the adjectives with admirable fluency.

Lily flashed her a sharp look. "All of the above," she confirmed unhappily. "He's also rich, powerful, arrogant—he runs people like Mussolini supposedly ran the Italian train system during World War Two."

"Don't you think that's a little unfair?" her friend challenged after a moment.

Lily sighed, rubbing her forehead. "Oh, I don't know. I suppose so," she admitted. "It's just that—well, if you want the truth, he keeps reminding me of my aunt."

There was a long silence. Paisley put down her wineglass and leaned forward, taking Lily's hands in hers. "Lily," she said, "if Dylan Chase reminds you of Amanda Wilding, you're not just confused, you're *sick.*"

Lily managed a wry smile. She pulled her hands free. "You know what I mean, Paisley."

"No, I don't," Paisley returned succinctly. "Explain it to me."

Lily sat back, curling her feet up under her. "Dylan is . . . is . . . he's—" she gestured helplessly. She'd been reacting instinctively for so long it was difficult to articulate what she was feeling. "Oh, don't you *see?* He's exactly the sort of man Aunt Amanda would have picked out for me!"

"What I see is that he's the man you've picked out for yourself," came the calm reply.

Lily felt her jaw drop. She shut it with a snap, feeling her heart thudding crazily in her chest. She hadn't yet dared to confront the truth of her feelings for Dylan in the silent, secret recesses of her heart. It was a shock to have it thrown in her face by someone else.

"Lily?" Paisley asked.

She looked at her friend. Her lungs seemed to be on the verge of requiring a course in remedial breathing. "I— I wouldn't say I picked him out," she countered. 'Picking out' implied she'd made some kind of conscious choice. She hadn't. Dylan Chase had just happened to her . . . the way the 1906 earthquake had just happened to San Francisco. She fiddled restlessly with a strand of her hair. "I . . . he wants me to go away with him this weekend," she said at last. "Some friends of his operate an inn on the Jersey shore. Cape May."

Something odd flickered through Paisley's eyes. "I know."

Lily stiffened. "You do? How?"

"Dylan asked me what was going to be on the schedule here at the playhouse."

"And when was this?"

"After the performance last Friday night," she said after a short hesitation. "While you were locking up the receipts."

"He didn't ask me to go away with him until Monday!"

"Well—"

"What did you tell him?"

"The truth. That we're going to be dark while we start making the changeover for *Sleeping Beauty in Space*. So, you're free to go."

Lily seriously doubted that she'd ever be free again if she *did* go. Two uninterrupted days in Dylan's company . . .

"What about my Saturday workshop?" she demanded.

Paisley rolled her eyes. "Oh, for heaven's sake! Give me a whip and a chair and a gun that shoots tranquilizing darts and I can handle that."

"Well—have you forgotten that we'd talked about working on the walls in the lobby? Now that we've got the money from the Chase Foundation—"

"Look, Lily, I understand how mixed-up you feel. Believe me, I do understand. But do you honestly expect me to believe you'd rather scrape plaster and spackle than spend two glorious days at some romantic seaside inn? That you'd turn down the chance to enjoy breakfast—and who knows what else—in bed with Dylan Chase—"

"Paisley!" She was torn between laughter and indignation at her friend's summation of her options.

"What?" Paisley's red hair seemed to bristle.

Lily threw up her hands. "When you put it like that—"

"I knew you'd come to your senses."

Lily wasn't at all sure that was what she'd done.

The place they went to was about a four-hour drive from Manhattan. On the way, Dylan filled Lily in a bit on the background of its owners. Paul Laurent, he explained, had once been one of the stars of ChaseCo's legal department. His wife, Nora, had been a successful advertising copywriter. Six years before, Paul had suffered a heart attack. Fortunately, it had been a very mild one; but it had prompted both of them to reevaluate their lives. One thing had led to another, and they'd wound up buying a rundown Victorian-period house on the Jersey shore, lovingly restoring it to its former Gothic Revival glory, and opening a bed-and-breakfast inn.

It was early Friday evening when they pulled up in front of the three-story house in Dylan's black Ferrari. The street was lined with sycamores. Although it was dark outside, there was enough illumination from the moon and streetlamps for Lily to form a very favorable impression of the inn's ivory, pale-blue, and black exterior.

"It's wonderful," she told Dylan, giving him a vivid smile of appreciation.

"I'm glad you like it," he returned, killing the engine. "It was pretty much of a lost cause when Nora and Paul bought it. But, thanks to a lot of hard work and a little creativity, they've turned it into something special. Nora likes to say this is one example of the Gothic style of architecture that had to be brought back from the *dead,* not just revived."

Lily laughed. "Whatever they did, it obviously worked. Do you think they'd be interested in trying their hand at a rundown theater?"

Dylan paused in the act of opening his door. He glanced at Lily. "I thought we'd agreed this was a weekend to get away from it all," he said lightly. He wanted her mind off the playhouse for a number of reasons.

"True," she conceded. "Sorry."

"Just don't let it happen again, Miss Bancroft."

"Anything you say, Mr. Chase."

"Anything?"

Lily smiled. "Oh, probably," she said.

"I hope you didn't mind the cross-examination over dinner," Dylan said quietly many hours later, nuzzling his mouth tenderly against Lily's temple.

Lily cuddled against him, her fingers drifting leisurely through the rough silk of his chest hair. "Mmm . . . no," she told him truthfully. Her answer was really little more than a contented sigh. She felt Dylan's warm breath eddy across her cheek. Turning her face a little, she pressed a soft kiss on the smoothly muscled curve of his naked shoulder.

Although their obvious curiosity about her and her relationship with Dylan had made Lily feel a bit awkward—as though she was on display in a spotlight—she'd found herself quickly drawn to the Laurents. Paul was a tall man in his mid-forties, with thinning salt-and-pepper hair, glasses, and a slow, deliberate way of speaking. Nora was three or four years younger, a great many inches shorter, and rather plain until she smiled.

"I've always come here on my own before," he commented after a few seconds, aware of the stirrings of desire low in his body. His fingers played teasingly over the sensitive underside of one of her breasts for a moment, then closed over the ripening globe of smooth flesh. "That's why you got so many questions."

Lily wasn't completely prepared for the glorious explosion of happiness Dylan's murmured words triggered inside her. It had been clear from Nora's and Paul's casual comments about his "regular" room and "favorite" foods that he'd come here fairly frequently in the past. Until this moment, she hadn't known how desperately she'd hoped he'd come alone.

"Lily?"

She didn't answer instantly. She had to wait until she was sure the star shower of relief she was feeling wouldn't show in her voice. Finally, she remarked: "You know, I don't think they believed the story of how we met."

"You mean the one that started: 'Once upon a time, Snow White went uptown in a taxi to seek her fortune'?"

"Mmm. It wasn't very nice of you to refer to Gary as the Clown Prince."

"Not nice, but accurate," Dylan responded. His

thoughts moved back fleetingly to what he knew must be going on in Manhattan at this very second. It was odd. While everybody else had accepted his forty-eight-hour transformation plan eagerly, Gary had reacted to the idea with a notable lack of enthusiasm. Dylan hadn't had time to sort out his younger brother's peculiar attitude before he'd left; he intended to do so when he returned.

"Well, it wasn't accurate to say I assaulted you with an apple," Lily quibbled with a laugh.

Dylan shoved all thoughts of Gary out of his mind. Shifting, he propped himself up on one elbow so he could look down at Lily's face. "Sweetheart, if my reflexes had been any slower, you would have been guilty of committing a felony in the *fruit* degree." He grinned, his teeth gleaming in the dim light. Beneath his partially lowered lids, his eyes glinted with dark fires.

Lily made a sound that was half-laugh, half-groan. "That kind of joke should be a *pun*ishable offense," she declared. Lifting one hand, she traced the strongly marked line of his dark brows, then skated the tip of her fingers lightly down his nose. She'd tried, over the past few weeks, to analyze his features one by one to discover why she found his face so compelling. She still hadn't succeeded in solving the puzzle.

Dylan stroked his palm up the line of her upper leg and hip, rocking it provocatively against the slender span of her waist. After a few seconds, he slipped his hand behind her, fingers splayed possessively, and pulled her to him. "You'd never get the charge to stand up in court," he told her, brushing his mouth against hers.

If Lily had ever had any doubts about the validity of the grade school science lesson that had taught her how friction creates heat, they would have been dispelled by the tiny flames that caressing contact sparked in her bloodstream. She parted her lips to accept the bold thrust of Dylan's tongue, then parried with a teasing feint of her own.

"Mmm . . ." Dylan broke the kiss at last. The throb of desire he'd felt earlier had grown to a steady pounding. His breathing was ragged, and he had the familiar feeling that the restraining bonds of his self-control were beginning to fray. "What do you want to do tomorrow?" he asked huskily.

Lily's eyes widened. *Tomorrow?* Why didn't he ask her what she wanted to do right now? "Umm, t-tomorrow? I— I don't have any plans. Sleep late, I suppose. Stay in bed." Moistening her lips with a darting lick of her tongue, she slanted him a deliberately alluring look through the screen of her lowered lashes. "What do *you* want to do, tomorrow, Dylan?" she asked huskily.

"Wake up early and stay in bed," came the immediate reply.

"Ah." She moved her hips sinuously, feeling the proud potency of his arousal. "Well, you have to go to sleep before you can wake up."

"That's generally the way it works," Dylan agreed. "There's just one little problem."

"Mmm . . . Dyl—yes! A—you said a little problem?" She sucked in a shuddery breath as she felt the search of his fingers against the aching bud of her feminine core. Her pulse was jumping as though her veins were no longer filled with blood but with millions of tiny creatures on miniature pogo sticks.

"Yes. You see, I'm not at all sleepy."

Lily wasn't either. But, by the time slumber finally claimed her, she was deliciously, deliriously exhausted.

"I think we may have made too much noise last night," Lily commented ruefully the next afternoon as she and Dylan walked hand in hand along a virtually deserted stretch of beach. Earlier in the day, they'd bicycled into town and spent a few hours exploring Cape May's Historic District.

"Oh? Why do you say that?" Dylan asked lazily. The sky overhead was a vivid, cloudless blue. The air was crisp and cool, with the clean tang of the Atlantic Ocean in it. He felt more relaxed than he had in months—no, years.

"You know Mr. Nathanson? The bald man who said he teaches nineteenth-century British literature?"

"The man in the room next to ours?"

"Yes. Did you see the look he gave us when we came downstairs for the breakfast buffet? And, after that, every time I looked up from my plate, he was *staring* at me."

Dylan laughed, swinging her hand. "Maybe he wasn't staring at *you*. Maybe he was staring at what was on your plate," he suggested teasingly.

Lily stopped. "What's that supposed to mean?" she demanded.

"You had a pretty impressive pile of food, Lily."

"A *pile?*"

"Eggs, bacon, and sausage. A grilled tomato. Hashed brown potatoes. Plus *two* cherry muffins and—"

"I was hungry!"

"Oh, really?"

"You should talk, Dylan. You're the one who ate three *piles* of apple pancakes."

"Stacks, sweetheart. The word is stacks."

"The word is piles, and they were drowning in butter and maple syrup."

"I have a—ah—very hearty appetite in the morning."

Green-gray eyes fused to amber-brown ones as Lily remembered, flushing, just how "hearty" both of their appetites had been shortly after dawn. "Yes, well, I—I still say Mr. Nathanson must have heard us," she said a little breathlessly. "I could certainly hear *him* this morning when he was clomping around on the other side of the wall."

"It's an inhibiting thought, isn't it?" Dylan remarked blandly. The expression in his eyes was anything but that.

Lily nodded, aware of a pleasant unfurling of sensation in her stomach. "A lot of old houses have that problem. Did you ever consider the possibility that lack of soundproofing was the real cause of all that repression during the Victorian era?"

Dylan outlined the generous curves of her lips with the tip of one finger, then painted the rosy flesh with the ball of his thumb. "No, I can't say that I have," he admitted. "But I *am* considering the possibility that Mr. Nathanson is still out visiting antique shops."

"Now *that's* a possibility worth considering."

"I'll race you back to the inn. You've still got at least one cherry muffin to run off."

"You know, I think I was wrong," Dylan said, closing his eyes on a sigh of absolute contentment.

"Well, this is a first," Lily returned, working up a lather with the cake of sweetly scented soap the inn had supplied. Smiling to herself with a secret sense of mischief, she began to wash Dylan's back.

He cracked open one eye and glanced over his shoulder. "Much as I hate to disillusion you, I have been wrong once or twice before this."

Lily laughed, massaging his sleek shoulders with a steady rhythm. The steamy-warm water in the bath lapped against her body. "Much as I hate to disillusion *you,* I had noticed. What I meant was that this is the first time I've ever heard you *admit* you were wrong."

"Ah."

"Well?"

"Well, what?"

"What were you wrong about?" She exerted a little pressure with her fingers.

"Oh. I used to think lounging in a Jacuzzi was the most enjoyable aquatic experience known to man. I've decided lounging in a claw-foot bathtub-built-for-two has that beat all to hell."

"You just like having your back washed," Lily retorted.

"Umm-hmm," he agreed, shifting himself around. He took the soap from her. "I also like washing other people's backs." His eyes dropped as he admired her pale, bubble-filmed breasts. The rosy tips began to pout in answer and invitation. "And fronts."

"Dylan—" He was like a bliss-inducing drug to her.

"Did I ever tell you I was on the swim team at school?"

Lily shook her head once, the sodden ends of her hair slapping damply against her heated, sensitive skin. "Freestyle?"

"Individual medley. Freestyle, backstroke, butterfly, and—ah, yes, you like that, Lily?"

"I did—I did some—ahhhh—synchronized s-swimming in school," she volunteered shakily.

"Good," he smiled heatedly. "Then you know that the real secret to water sports is to just dive right in."

"Ahh—yes! *Dylan!*"

Her hands flew up in a splash of water. Lily locked them around his neck and clung to him. Otherwise, she would have drowned in the tidal wave of pleasure that broke over her.

"You were right about Mr. Nathanson, Lily."

"Oh?"

"When we passed him on the stairs just now, he gave us a very strange look."

"I've got news for you, Dylan. He wasn't giving *us* anything. He was staring at you. No—he was *smelling* you."

"Excuse me?"

"You remember the soap I used to wash your back and you used to wash my—ah—whatever? It was perfumed."

"Lily, my love, after dinner—once I get my strength back—I am going to get you for this."

"Promises. Promises.

My love. Somehow, that casually voiced endearment kept echoing in Lily's mind. It was still echoing early the next morning when she woke. Dylan was asleep, his breathing easy and measured, his features softened into something close to vulnerability. His tall, tempered body was warm against hers. She stroked a butterfly-light finger along his arm, observing yet again the contrast in their coloring. Lily knew now that, except for a narrow band of pale skin around his lean hips, Dylan was tanned all over. On the rare occasions when he allowed himself to relax, the "Lone Wolf of Wall Street" evidently had a jungle cat's appreciation of the hedonistic pleasures of stretching out under the sun.

My love. She didn't know whether he'd meant those two words when he'd said them. She didn't even know if he'd thought about saying them.

She'd been thinking them . . . meaning them . . . for longer than she wanted to admit. But she didn't know if she'd ever be able to say them.

My love. For no rational reason, her mind arrowed back to the expression she'd seen on Dylan's face after the first time he'd kissed her. She'd thought he looked like a man who'd found something he'd been searching for, but discovered it was not at all what he'd expected.

Lily Bancroft understood that feeling with every fiber of her being.

"You know, weekend getaways have been known to last through Monday," Nora Laurent said invitingly as Lily and Dylan prepared to take their leave.

"Sounds good to me." Lily nodded, giving Dylan a flirtatious smile.

"It sounds good to me, too," Dylan agreed. "But we've got to get back to the city." He didn't really want to leave. But responsibilities beckoned. Besides, he was anxious to see how Lily was going to react to what had been accomplished in her absence.

"Do we have to?" Lily asked, doing a perfect imitation of Kerri Phillips in one of her remarkably rare moments of rebellion against "Uncle Dylan."

Dylan's mouth twisted. "Yes, we have to," he returned. "We've got to go back so you can get your surprise."

"Surprise?" Lily asked, startled. "What surprise?"

"If I told you, it wouldn't be a surprise. You'll have to wait until we get back to Manhattan to find out."

"But that's a four-hour wait!" Lily protested.

"I'll drive fast."

"Dylan, you can't just drop something like that and not say anything else," Nora declared, weighing in on Lily's side.

"Yes, he can," her husband informed her.

"At least give me a *hint,*" Lily demanded.

Dylan shook his head decisively. "I want this to be a complete surprise."

- 7 -

It was more than a complete surprise. It was a total shock.

Lily got an inkling of what awaited her when they drove up in front of the Potluck Playhouse shortly after dusk and she noticed that its modest marquee was no longer listing slightly to the right. The sign, which declared that *Sleeping Beauty in Space* was "Opening This Friday" was absolutely level. What was more, all of the lights that bordered it were on and working. There were none of the usual burned-out bulbs.

"Dylan—?" she began questioningly, her eyes searching his face. A seed of suspicion appeared in what had been the perfect garden of happiness this past weekend had created within her.

"You'll see," he said with a smile. "I think Paisley and Sam should be waiting inside."

The seed took root when Lily saw that smile. It was a pleasant smile. A charming, warm, and even tender smile. But it was also tinged with what she could only, unhappily, define as smugness.

Paisley and Sam were waiting inside. They were standing—petite, graceful mother next to tall, gawky son—in the middle of the lobby. The lobby smelled of fresh paint and new carpet. It gleamed. They were both grinning.

"Surprise!" they sang out.

Lily set her suitcase down very, very carefully. "What—what happened?" she asked. She didn't dare look at Dylan.

"Everything!" Sam exulted.

He was exaggerating, of course, but only a little. By the time Paisley got through showing Lily the changes that had been made since Friday afternoon, Lily couldn't help wondering what *hadn't* happened to the playhouse—to *her* playhouse, damn it!

"—that perpetually leaking pipe is fixed," Paisley said, ticking down the list. "So there's no more worrying about waterlogged props."

"And do you believe that upholstery?" Sam chimed in. "Deluxe comfort! People will be willing to pay more for seats just because they'll be so great to sit in!"

"And the new curtain system is supposed to get here before the opening of *Sleeping Beauty in Space,"* Paisley added.

"But how—?" Lily got out, gesturing around her. She felt as though she'd been blown up into a million pieces and she was struggling to put herself back together. She didn't need to ask *whom*. That was obvious. Dylan. Dylan had done it. Without asking her. Without saying a word. He'd just done it.

"Oh, it was incredible, Lily," Sam assured her, then went blithely on to confirm her suspicions. "Dylan arranged it so the first crew would get here right after you left. And then— Hey!" he broke off, his eyes ping-ponging back and forth between them. "Did you guys have a good time?"

"Yes, Sam," Dylan said tersely. Half of him was surveying the renovations that had been done and the changes that had been made with the same cool, critical eye he used to evaluate any job carried out on his orders. The other half—notably less cool—was trying to get a fix on Lily's reaction. Dylan thought she looked stunned. And he wasn't at all sure it was stunned in the positive sense, either. She'd only met his gaze once since they'd walked in, and he hadn't been able to begin sorting out the wildly contradictory emotions he'd seen swirling in the depths of her changeable eyes. "We had a very good time."

"Yeah, I figured you would," Sam returned. The grin that lit up his freckled face wasn't quite as knowing as he obviously thought it was. "Anyways, Lily, like I was saying. Dylan fixed it for the first crew to come in Friday afternoon. And as soon as their shift ended, another crew came in, and then another. I mean, we are talking about completely around the clock! No stopping. The last guys didn't quit until—oh—practically right before you got back. You should have been here."

"Yes," Lily agreed. "I should have."

"Lily—" Paisley began, her own excitement clearly tempered by her puzzlement at Lily's manner.

Lily glanced at her friend. Her friend who had known all about this and said nothing. "What happened to my Saturday workshop?" she asked without inflection.

"Mom canceled that," Sam answered promptly. "Geez, can you imagine letting the Kamikaze Twins loose in a place filled with electric drills and power saws?"

"I don't think our liability insurance covers anything

like that," his mother commented wryly. "Ah—well, now that we've had the grand tour . . . I think there might be some champagne up in your refrigerator, Lily."

"I'm sure there is," she replied. And she was sure. Dylan Chase was the type of man who thought of everything. Even the champagne for toasting yet another Chase success.

"Great!" Sam enthused. "I'll bet everybody feels like a celebration, huh?"

Green-gray eyes collided with amber-brown ones so hard following this innocent but unfelicitously worded question that Lily was astounded no one heard the sound of a crash.

"All right," Dylan said quietly, turning back to face Lily after closing the door on the departing Paisley and Sam Stevens. "Do you want to tell me what's wrong?"

Lily was sitting on the sofa, her hands folded in her lap, her posture faultlessly, self-consciously erect. "Why do you want to know? So you can tell me what to do about it?"

He vaguely recognized the paraphrase of the artless remarks his niece had made that Sunday after the matinee of *Hansel and Gretel Go Hollywood*. But why would—? "Lily—" he started.

"And what makes you think there's anything wrong in the first place?"

He exhaled on a short, sharp breath and closed the distance between them in six or seven long, lithe strides. "You mean aside from the fact that you'd be a lot more approachable wrapped in barbed wire than you seem to be right now?" he shot back. What the hell was the matter? Gripping her by her forearms, he hauled her to a standing position. "Damn it, Lily, don't be coy with me. Not now."

She jerked herself free. "Fine, I won't be coy. I'll lay it on the line. All I want to know is: How dare you do what you've done to my theater? What makes you think you have the right—"

"Right? Lily, I talked to Paisley—"

"But you didn't talk to me!"

Dylan shook his head, trying to make sense of the anger and the hurt and the—what? could it be disillusionment?—he felt emanating from her. He wasn't expecting any great show of gratitude for what he'd done. He'd seen a problem; he'd had the power to solve it, so he had. That was his way. He didn't want Lily to feel indebted to him. But he had thought she'd appreciate his actions, not attack him for them.

"Are you upset because you feel I went behind your back?" he asked, searching for some reasonable explanation. "If you are, I'm sorry. But I wanted this to be a surprise—"

"Well, you certainly got what you wanted!"

"For godsake, everything I had done this weekend was what you'd told me you were going to do—"

"Yes!" she interrupted, glaring at him. "*I* was going to do. The *Potluck Playhouse* was going to do. Who asked you?"

Flicked on the raw, his immediate instinct was to hit back. "You asked my family's foundation for money. And got it, I might add."

Lily flinched. "And you think that makes it all right for you to take over?" she asked in a strained voice. What was that proverb her Aunt Amanda had been so fond of quoting? Oh, yes: *He who pays the piper, calls the tune*. An appalling thought hit her. "Are you the reason our grant got approved?"

He hesitated.

"Are you?" It would change everything between

them—irrevocably, irredeemably—if he were.

"No," he replied flatly. "The Potluck Playhouse was endorsed for foundation funding on its own merits."

"But?" she challenged. There was something more. She could see it in his eyes.

"But I did intervene to speed up the paperwork," he informed her. "So?"

She stared at him. "So . . . we owe you, don't we? And what you had done this weekend, what was that? Building up our—*my*—indebtedness to you?" Lord, how many times during her first years in Boston had she been reminded what she "owed" her Aunt Amanda? Whenever she displeased or disobeyed, her debt to her wealthy and powerful relative had been trotted out as a reproach. And later, as she'd gotten older, she'd been told over and over about what she "owed" the Wilding family name and position.

"That—" For a moment, Dylan's fury at what he thought she was suggesting strangled his ability to speak. He tamped down his temper to a barely controllable level by sheer force of will. *"That is not fair, Lily, and you know it."*

"Do I? Yes, we were planning to make renovations . . . repairs . . . we were going to do everything you had —*ordered*—done. But not all at once! Do you think I don't know what carpeting, audience seats, curtains, and so on cost? To say nothing of the price of around-the-clock union labor? Even *with* the grant, we can't afford that!"

For a moment, he was torn between anger and admiration. Dylan was so accustomed to having people depend on him, to having them take, take, take, that he wasn't entirely sure how to cope with the driven, defensive independence that underlay every word Lily was throwing at him. Her obvious determination to stand on her own two feet was immensely dear to him. But it was also damnably infuriating to him because, deep down, he knew that he wanted to sweep her *off* her two feet.

"Forget about the cost, the price, the money," he commanded. "I can afford—" He broke off, cursing his own stupidity even before he fully registered the desolate anger in her eyes. "Lily—" he started urgently.

Lily was standing absolutely still, but she felt as though she was trembling like a leaf in a windstorm. "That's the bottom line for you, isn't it, Dylan? What you can afford? Which is just about anything or anyone—"

"No, dammit!" He caught her shoulders roughly. "It's not— No, I am not going to let you go! Look, I can't pretend to completely understand this hang-up you have about money. But I do understand enough to know that you're hardly a poverty case. I also understand that you've got the kind of social poise you don't pick up on the wrong side of the tracks in northwest Nowhere."

"Dylan—" Lily had stopped struggling, but not resisting.

"Let me finish." He shook her once, then moderated both his tone and grip. "Lily, if I were trying to buy you—and that *is* what you're accusing me of, isn't it?—I sure as hell would make my opening bid a lot higher than a coat of paint for a lobby, a curtain system for a pint-sized stage, and a bunch of chairs! You may not believe anything else, but believe that." He paused for a moment, watching her carefully. It seemed to him that the condemnation in her eyes had softened to questioning. When he continued, his voice was soft but intense. "You've told me how much you care about the Potluck Playhouse. About how committed you are to what goes on there. Can't you accept that I might want a chance to share in that caring and commitment just a little bit?"

She wanted to believe him. Desperately. But it was so *hard!* "I don't—"

He saw her confusion, her uncertainty. "If a stranger walked in off the street and handed you a check for a million dollars for the Potluck Playhouse, you'd probably take it. Right? Or if Sam Stevens made a killing in the stock market and decided to spread the capital gains around, you'd probably take his money, too. Then why can't you take something from me?"

"It's not the same!" It was a cry from her heart.

"Why not? Because we're lovers?"

She made a movement with her head. She didn't know whether she was nodding it or shaking it. What could she say to him? That she loved him, but that ten years of experience had made her desperately afraid of being in the power of anyone with his ability to overwhelm and control?

"Lily—" He let go of her shoulders and brought his hands up, cradling her face in his palms. "I won't deny that I did what I did in the hope of pleasing you. I wanted to . . . give you a gift that meant something. Maybe it's my failing that I tend to show what I feel with material things . . . rather than less tangible gestures. But that's the way I am." He stroked her cheeks tenderly, compellingly. "Trust me enough to accept what I want to give—and the way I give it." He waited for a few seconds then added: *"Please."*

Lily gazed up at him. His touch was so sure, and yet gentle. And there was something very moving—something almost vulnerable—about the utter honesty of his plea.

Trust him? She didn't know if she ever could . . . completely. But *love* him. She knew she already did . . . absolutely.

She accepted Dylan's gifts—all of them— with a kiss.

"Lily?" It was much, much later and they lay on her bed. They were pressed flesh to flesh, skin to skin, heart to heart.

"Mmm." Lily hardly dared speak. She felt as though they'd created something with their lovemaking so infinitely precious, yet so exquisitely fragile in its newness, that a single wrong word—even too harsh a thought—might shatter it.

"Are you ever going to tell me what all of that was really about?" he inquired softly, his breath stirring her hair.

Lily sighed. What they'd made between them didn't break at the sound of a human voice after all. It remained constant—shimmering, glimmering, full of hope.

"Soon," she promised with her lips. *My love,* she added in her heart.

"Soon" came three nights later.

They were attending one of Manhattan's most glittering charity balls, at one of Manhattan's most glittering hotels. It was the kind of event that kept couturiers, jewelers, and hair stylists in business, gave news-hungry gossip columnists something to write about, and (incidentally, Lily knew some cynics suggested) raised money for a worthy cause.

Lily sensed Dylan was surprised that she'd agreed to go with him, although he didn't press her for reasons. She wasn't certain she could have given him any if he had.

"So, tonight you're Cinderella, right?" Gary Chase suggested with an affectionately teasing grin as he whirled her around the dance floor.

"No, tonight I'm just plain Lily Bancroft," Lily returned. It was remarkable how easily old skills came back. She hadn't waltzed in *years,* and yet, here she was, swooped and gliding without a single misstep or trod-upon toe. Obviously, you could take the girl out of the Saturday afternoon ballroom dancing class, but you couldn't take the Saturday afternoon ballroom dancing class out of the girl.

"Plain?" Gary mocked. "Have you looked in a mirror this evening?"

Lily simply smiled. She hadn't glanced at a mirror since leaving her loft hours before. She hadn't needed to, really. What she'd seen reflected Dylan's eyes each time he'd looked at her tonight made her feel consummately beautiful.

Her dress was a simple, long-sleeved sluice of hammered satin so darkly, richly green that it looked almost black. The front of the gown was utterly plain and had a high neck. The back dipped to a low, softly draped V. Her strappy sandals were of bronze kid as was her tiny evening purse. She'd pulled her hair back into a smooth, tight chignon.

In some ways, there was validity to Gary's Cinderella remark. She'd had some help in getting to tonight's ball from three "fairy godmothers." Her makeup was courtesy of Joelle Peters, who had called up two decades of theatrical experience to enhance Lily's matte pale skin, wide-set eyes, and generous mouth. Her gold and emerald earrings were on loan from Paisley. Her wrap for the evening—a black velvet cape—had been borrowed, too. Anthea, the avant-garde artist-turned-set-designer, had only been too happy to contribute it to the cause.

"I don't suppose you'd consider running off with me," Gary mused.

"I did that once, actually," Lily replied, almost without thinking.

"Did what?"

"Ran off with someone."

"What happened?"

She looked at him, unable to help comparing him with his older brother. Gary looked attractive in his tuxedo, but Dylan was the devastating epitome of male elegance in the black and white severity of his. Gary, she'd noticed this evening, seemed well-enough liked by everyone; he was charming and funny, if a little immature on occasion. Dylan, on the other hand, was quietly sought out by the movers and the shakers of the city. He commanded respect and deferential attention, even from men twenty years his senior.

And yet, Lily reflected, there were flashes every now and then—barely hints, really—that there were unplumbed complexities lurking beneath Gary's decidedly uncomplicated exterior.

"Lily," Gary interrupted her train of thought in a wry tone.

Lily started, almost losing the rhythm of the music. "Sorry," she apologized quickly.

"Never mind that. What happened with you and the guy you ran off with?"

"Oh. We—we failed to live happily ever after."

"Ah." The waltz came to an end in a polite rustle of applause. "Well, if *I* want to live at all ever after—much less happily—I'd better get you back to Dylan," Gary declared cheerfully. "Much as I enjoy the feeling of having something my big brother wants, I know when to stop pushing my luck."

With that, Gary escorted Lily back to Dylan, traded a few quips with his brother, and ambled off in pursuit of some other amusement.

Dylan had been standing with a well-known magazine publisher and his wife and one of the country's highest-powered lawyers and his longtime ladyfriend while Lily had her dance with Gary. He was conscious of a niggling jealousy as he watched them together, laughing and talking. Damn, why did she have to seem so completely open with him? Why did she seem to trust his younger brother where she didn't trust him?

Perhaps tonight would change all that. Dylan intended to ask Lily to marry him tonight. He wanted her, needed her . . . loved her. And he was going to tell her so.

He had the ring back at his apartment. He'd taken it out of his safety deposit box at the bank Monday morning. The ring was an inheritance from his grandfather. It had belonged to *his* mother—Dylan's great-grandmother. The setting was very old-fashioned, and Dylan had debated about having it reset. Ultimately, he'd decided the one-of-a-kind combination of diamonds and emeralds probably would appeal to Lily.

He devoutly hoped so. But if it didn't, he'd have the ring redesigned. Or he'd buy her something completely new, if that's what she wanted. Hell, she could choose a trinket out of a Cracker Jack box for an engagement ring as long as she agreed to become his wife!

"Did you have a good time with Gary?" he asked her as his brother walked away.

Lily smiled, her pulse giving a curious lurch as she saw a flashing surge of possessiveness and determination in Dylan's eyes. "Oh, yes," she told him lightly. "He asked me to run away with him, in fact."

Dylan's brows lifted. "I hope you turned him down. I don't think you'd like to have my brother's broken kneecaps on your conscious."

This was greeted by general laughter from the other two couples. When it faded, Dylan performed the necessary introductions. For the dozenth or so times that evening, he was struck by how at ease Lily seemed in a situation that, on the surface, was very different from what she was used to in the East Village.

It was interesting, Lily reflected, following the conversation with only half an ear, how she had retained the ability to make polite social chitchat—as well as dance the waltz. It was all a matter of nodding, smiling, and occasionally dropping the right name. In fact—

"Lily? Lily Bancroft?"

There are some voices that stick in the memory—or, in this particular case, the throat. It had been more than nine years since Lily had heard this voice, or the affected squeal of joyous recognition that punctuated the exclamation of her name, but she knew exactly whom both belonged to.

With an awful sense of resignation, and a miserable awareness of a sudden alertness in Dylan, Lily turned around.

"Oooooh!" Kiki—short for Kirkland—Winslow squealed again, indulging in the right-cheek-left-cheek air kiss she'd developed in boarding school. "I just knew it was you, darling! It's been absolutely *forever!* After all these years! How positively divine! This is my husband, Brinsley Pruitt. Bink, darling, this is Lily Bancroft. We knew each other ages ago back in Boston. Why, we were just like *sisters!* We went to boarding school together. And we made our debut the same year at the Cotillion—isn't that right, Lily? And she utterly *crushed* my poor brother, Kip, when she ran off and married some boy from—from—where was he from, darling?"

"Springfield," Lily supplied numbly. How could she have crushed Kip—short for Carter—Winslow the Fourth? She'd never even gone out with him! She couldn't even recall what he looked like. All she had was a dim memory of her Aunt Amanda—

"Oh, yes, *Springfield.*" Kiki pronounced the name as though it might he contagious. "You see, Bink—and I know you were absolutely in the dark about this, Lily—Lily's Aunt Amanda and Daddy had their hearts *set* on Kip and Lily getting together. Sort of a merger between banks, you see. Lily's a Wilding, you understand. Mother's side. But, well, it all went *poof*"—Kiki waved her exquisitely manicured hands and tens of thousands of dollars worth of diamonds around expressively.

"Ah—Kiki—" Lily took a deep breath. "I'd like you to meet my—Dylan Chase. Dylan, this is Kiki—Kirkland—Winslow Pruitt. And her husband, ah—Brinsley."

Everyone did the polite thing. Everyone went on doing the polite thing for about ten minutes until Dylan, whose retentive memory had unleashed a wealth of information in response to the name *Wilding*, suddenly looked at his watch and cleared his throat. "You're going to have to excuse us," he said smoothly, slipping an arm around Lily. He could feel the tension in her slender body. "I'm afraid Lily and I must be leaving. Mitch and Anne—" He nodded to the publisher and his wife. "Ted and Leona." Another nod, this one shared between the lawyer and his companion. "And Kiki and Brinsley. Good to see you all. Enjoy the rest of the evening."

Everyone murmured politely one last time, and Dylan led Lily away.

"Dylan—" she began as he maneuvered her through the well-dressed, well-known throng with ruthless efficiency. No one—*nothing*—was allowed to impede their progress for long.

"We'll talk when we get to my apartment," he said.

Her stomach turned over. Oh God, she knew—*she knew*—he'd absorbed all the implications of the Wilding name. "I didn't want you to find out like this, Dylan," she told him sincerely, desperately.

He heard the turbulence in her voice. He wondered if she had any idea of the kind of turmoil he was feeling at this moment. "It's all right," he said.

"But about what Kiki said. I don't want you to think—"

He smiled. The expression felt savage. "Don't worry, love. I don't for a second think you and Kiki Winslow Pruitt were like sisters ages ago back in Boston. I'm not even sure you're in the same species."

The ride back to his apartment was silent. So was the ride in the private elevator to his duplex. After relieving her of her black velvet cloak and disposing of his own dark overcoat, Dylan led her into the library. He closed his mind to the mental image of the small velvet-covered box sitting on the table next to his bed.

"Do you want a drink, Lily?" he asked softly as he watched her sink gracefully onto one of the two couches flanking the fireplace.

Lily shook her head, looking around. She loved this room, with its deep, rich red walls and its clean, classic furnishings. She loved the eclectic collection of books—books chosen, she knew, to be read and reread, not to establish some cultural or intellectual credentials. She also loved the starkly simple beauty of the pieces of black-on-black American Indian pottery scattered about.

She and Dylan had made love once in this room, on the Oriental rug in front of the black marble fireplace.

"Are you sure?" he pressed. Lord, she looked pale. And more than a little shattered. But then, he supposed running headlong into a past you'd been trying to evade would tend to have that kind of effect.

"Positive," Lily told him.

"All right. But I'm going to have one."

"Good," she murmured.

There was a pause, broken only by the sound of ice clinking against glass and the splash of expensive Scotch being poured with a generous hand. Lily watched Dylan fix his drink, take a deep taste of it, then walk slowly over to the couch where she was sitting. After a moment, he sat down next to her. He sat close enough so she could reach out and touch him, but not so close that she felt crowded.

"So," he said, jerking his tie loose. "Tell me, Lily."

She did. All of it. Everything. It came pouring out of her in a tumbling rush of words, memories, and undisguised emotions. She told him about her mother. Her father. The car crash just a month after her tenth birthday. She told him about her Aunt Amanda. About how a dazed, grief-stricken child had sought some security, some semblance of love, by trying to bow to the autocratic will of an unbending woman thirty years her senior. And about how that same child had eventually rebelled rather than be broken to the mold of Wilding expectations.

She told him about Howard Davis, Junior, and her three-year marriage to him.

In the end, she almost told Dylan Chase she'd fallen in love with him, but she held back at the last instant . . . uncertain.

There was another pause then, longer than the one that had come before Lily had begun to speak. Lily gazed at Dylan, then looked down at her knotted fingers, then glanced back at Dylan again. *Why didn't he say something?*

Dylan took a deep breath. He expelled it slowly. Lily had trusted him. Opened up to him. Lowered her defenses . . . completely. But, in doing so, she'd made it impossible for him to proclaim his love or his desire to marry her.

Dylan could have—would have—proclaimed both, if she hadn't told him her secrets. But knowing the truth about her as he now did . . .

Lily had run away from ten years of her life. Ten years that, no matter how she might try to deny it, had left an indelible mark on her. Until she reconciled herself to that, to the experiences that had, for better or for worse, shaped her, she'd remain a captive of the very past she wanted to escape.

"Dylan?" she whispered finally, unable to take the silence or the brooding power of his assessing stare anymore.

He set down his drink. He hadn't taken so much as a sip of it since she'd started speaking. The ice was completely melted.

"I—I almost wish you hadn't told me," he said quietly. His amber-brown eyes were very still, very steady, as they met her tumultuous green-gray ones.

Lily felt as though her heart was being squeezed by some inexorably closing vice. "It makes such a difference?"

"No!" He reacted instinctively, bringing his hands up to catch and cup her shoulders. "No, not in the way you mean."

"But—"

"Lily, you are who you are and what you are. The fact that your middle name happens to be Wilding doesn't matter to me." But it matters to you, my love, he added silently. And until you come to terms with that, what you've told me tonight *is* going to make a tremendous difference—to our future.

The vice opened. "Oh, Dylan. I was afraid—"

He drew her to him. "I know."

For a few minutes, it felt utterly right to rest against him, to rely on him. It was bliss to be held by him, to feel the soothing stroke of his fingers in her hair, to hear the rich, low murmur of his voice in her ear. He was so strong . . . so protective . . .

Too strong, something inside her said suddenly, warningly. *Too* protective.

Lily started to stiffen.

Dylan let her go instantly. He didn't want to, but he did. He knew Lily faced enough of a battle trying to fight herself. She didn't need the burden of trying to fight him as well. And she would have, if he'd tried to hang on to her.

Lily stared at him. She felt as though she were trying to balance on some ever-shifting razor's edge—that she was tiptoeing along a gossamer-fine tightrope with exhaustion on one side and exhilaration on the other. The sensation made her dizzy.

"It's all right, Lily," he told her. It was a reassurance for the moment, and a promise for the future.

"You do understand, don't you." It wasn't so much a question as a statement of dawning conviction.

"Oh, yes." He understood what he had to do. And, as in every other situation, he was going to do it.

She gave him a smile of incredible sweetness.

"Do you want to stay?" he asked, brushing a few stray strands of shiny brown hair off her forehead. She was so precious to him. So special.

She wanted to, but she knew she shouldn't. "I think —I think I should go home tonight."

He allowed himself one last touch, drinking in the texture of her skin with his fingertips. Dipping his head, he took one swift kiss. "I'll have Rodgers drive you."

That night, Dylan put the small velvet-covered box in the wall safe in his bedroom. He was determined it would not stay there long.

The next morning, he placed a phone call to Boston. When he finally reached the person he wanted, his opening words were unflinchingly straightforward: "Miss Wilding, my name is Dylan Chase, and I want to talk with you about your niece, Lily."

Eight hours later, he stood at a gate at LaGuardia International Airport and greeted Amanda Wilding—of the Boston banking Wildings—as she got off a plane.

- 8 -

"PAISLEY," LILY SAID, examining her friend's hopeless expression with a mixture of amusement and concern. "Is there anything I can get for you before I go?"

"A Valium," came the doleful reply. "No, two Valiums. Or maybe a Scotch. A triple Scotch."

Paisley was slumped in the center seat of the refurbished front row of the Potluck Playhouse, her director's clipboard in her blue-jeaned lap and her gray eyes fixed dully on the stage before her. She'd been sitting there, red hair drooping, radiating gloom, for the past thirty minutes. It was roughly five hours before the opening performance of *Sleeping Beauty in Space*.

Lily sat down next to her. "Paisley, we go through this every single time we open a new production. You spend twenty-four hours moping around, brooding about laying an egg, and knowing perfectly well that everything is going to be just terrific. And it always is. The Potluck Playhouse has never had a flop."

"There's always a first time. We're on the verge of a major theatrical fiasco, Lily. I can feel it in my bones."

"To the best of my knowledge, your bones have never been right about anything."

Paisley fixed her with a jaundiced eye. "It's fine for you to go floating around here like you're full of helium. You're going to high tea at the Plaza with a handsome prince. I like your dress, by the way. You should wear that shade of brown more often. It's sort of a cross between cinnamon toast and dark honey."

"Thank you, Paisley." Lily laughed. "I suppose I am a little high on happiness at the moment. Ever since I told Dylan the truth—I can't tell you how I feel!" She hadn't seen Dylan since their talk in his library—he'd had some sort of emergency the day before—but they'd spoken on the phone several times. Simply hearing his voice say her name made her tingle and melt. She loved him so much! "But, look, about this frenzy you're working yourself into—"

"This is not a frenzy. Don't you know incipient catatonia when you see it?"

"Oh, for heaven's sake! Did you used to act this way before opening nights when you were dancing on Broadway?" Lily demanded.

"No, I used to throw up before opening nights when I was dancing on Broadway. But I can't do that now. I'm a director. A director is expected to have dignity."

"I see. And you think doing an imitation of the Black Hole of Calcutta is dignified?" Lily wasn't really worried about her friend. She knew from experience that Paisley would revert to her usual bouncy self once the first-act curtain went up.

"You don't understand," Paisley accused her morosely.

"I understand that the dress rehearsal went—"

"No! Don't say it!"

"Paisley, the dress rehearsal went *wonderfully!*"

"Don't you know that a wonderful dress rehearsal is a sure sign of a disastrous opening performance?"

"The dress rehearsal for *Hansel and Gretel Go Hollywood* went off without a hitch, too, and its first night was terrific," Lily reminded her.

"Okay, okay, so there's an occasional exception to the rule."

"Do you want me to cancel my tea with Dylan?" Lily asked.

"No, no," Paisley refused immediately. "You'd be miserable if you did. Or, if you weren't miserable, you'd be beaming like Anthea's idiotic laser thing and that'd make *me* even more miserable than I already am. Go to the Plaza."

"Are you worried about the laser? I think Sam's friends from school have pulled off a pretty amazing effect."

"Amazing, hah!"

"They got an A on it from their independent-study adviser. And it's worked perfectly the last six times they've fired it."

"What about the *first* six times?"

"Well, not even Einstein scored one hundred percent."

"Einstein did not perform in front of New York theater critics and paying customers!"

"Paisley—"

"Go to the Plaza, Lily. Maybe I'll get lucky and the laser thing will blow up. That way we can cancel the show and save ourselves an incredible amount of professional humiliation."

Lily didn't really float up the steps of the Plaza Hotel, but she did come close to skipping. Her heart was overflowing with happiness. She felt it must be radiating out of the pores of her skin.

When he'd invited her for tea—something that struck Lily as irresistibly romantic—Dylan had said he had something important to talk with her about. He'd refused to tell her what it was, but his tone had sparked a bonfire of hope within her.

God, she loved him! And, deep inside, she believed he loved her, too. Could that be—?

"Madam?"

Lily started. She'd made it to the Palm Court without even registering the bustle of the busy but gracious lobby she'd moved through. She looked at the hotel staffer blankly for a moment and then realized what he was asking. "Oh—I'm joining someone here for tea," she explained quickly. Glancing beyond the neat, politely inquiring man, she spotted the face she wanted to see most in the world. "And there he is," she added.

"Of course, madam."

"Thank you."

Dylan rose, lean and tall in his navy business suit, as Lily began walking toward his table. The brilliant smile he directed at her from across the room made Lily feel as though she were in a spotlight. She wanted to bask in the glow of it. His eyes seemed to embrace her hungrily, their gold-glinting depths inviting her to share his passion.

Lily did share it. She knew the almost pagan power of the body hidden beneath the civilized, sophisticated veneer of custom tailoring and its elegant accoutrements. She knew the proud set of his head and shoulders . . . the strength of his arms and long legs . . . the fluid muscularity of his back . . . the arrogant, undeniable potency of his maleness. She knew every inch of him, every response. In that way, he was as much hers as she was his, and she reveled in their mutual possession.

She was so caught up in the storm of feelings Dylan was evoking in her—had evoked in her from the start—that it wasn't until she was barely a yard away from his table that she realized he wasn't alone.

Watching her approach intently, being stirred as he always was by her supple, sensual grace, Dylan saw the sudden change in her expression and bearing. And he knew to the split second when she comprehended what he had done.

He also knew that in doing it, he had committed a disastrous—possibly irreparable—mistake.

"Lily—" he started, appalled by what he was seeing. He'd expected a strong reaction—but this? She'd gone white and her eyes blazed with a wild, angry hurt. Yet, she didn't break down. Except for that one faltering instant of comprehension she maintained her poise. Dignity encased her like an impenetrable mantle of stone.

"Aunt Amanda," she said very quietly, very carefully, as though the act of saying the two words might tear her throat.

"Lily," Amanda Janaway Wilding greeted her niece. "It's been a long time."

"A lifetime." Had her aunt changed? Lily couldn't tell. The perfectly coiffed short hair was a little whiter, she thought. And there were more lines around the green-gray eyes. But the ramrod erect, never-touch-the-back-of-a-chair posture was still unchanged, as was the cool air of control. Amanda Wilding still favored good suits in dark, definite colors, suits that were made to last and worn for years. She also still carried a Hermès handbag and wore a triple strand of perfectly matched pearls around her throat.

"Lily—" Dylan tried again. "Why don't you—"

"Sit down?" she cut in, her voice like a razor blade. How could he have done this? *How?* "No, thank you. I'm not staying. Good-bye, Dylan. Aunt Amanda—"

she swallowed hard. "I didn't bother to tell you good-bye when I left to marry Howie. So, this is for then . . . and now. Good-bye."

Ten years of deportment lessons and a sense of pride kept her from running as she turned and walked toward the exit of the Palm Court. Nothing could have kept her from doing so once she reached the hotel lobby.

Dylan had let Lily Bancroft go once before, rejecting the impulse that had spurred at him to chase her down and kiss her senseless. Stunned as he was, he had no intention of letting her go again—*ever.*

"Miss Wilding—" Lily's aunt sat frozen across from Dylan.

The older woman shook her head. Her eyes looked unfocused and her fingers weren't steady as she opened her fine black calfskin handbag. "I'm all right. Go."

Dylan did.

He caught up with Lily at the top of the wide gray stone stairs that led up to the Plaza's Fifth Avenue entrance. Ignoring the astonished stares of several people going into the hotel, Dylan grabbed Lily and swung her around to face him. The abruptness of the movement made her long, loose hair fan out in a swirl of tawny silk.

"You are not leaving," he told her.

"Just watch me!" Lily tried to pull herself free but failed. Even with the cushioned barrier of the lined sleeve of her raincoat and her other clothes, the grip of his fingers on her flesh was bruising.

"I am not letting you go, Lily."

"You can't tell me what to do, Dylan!" she spat at him, eyes blazing. "Can't you get that through your arrogant skull? I don't care if you're the all-powerful captain of commerce who buys and sells anything and everything he wants. I don't care if you're the all-knowing head of the Chase family who solves everybody's problems. You don't own *me!* You don't run *my* life! You don't—"

"Damn it, Lily! I love you and I want to marry you!"

It was the declaration he'd intended to make, but not, God knew, the way he'd intended to make it. He'd never said those words to a woman before. He'd wanted to offer them to Lily, to say them to her for the first time, in tenderness, in passion, and in private. Instead, he'd just flung them at her like a bunch of rocks, tossing them in her face in one of the most public settings imaginable.

Stunned by the force of Dylan's words, Lily tried to grapple with the meaning of what he'd just said. *He wanted to marry her?* He'd given no hint, showed no sign of that before this. Why *now?* What could have—? Then it hit her, horribly.

"Tell me," she began painfully. "How soon after Kiki said the name Wilding did you decide you wanted to marry me?"

Dylan let go of her, because he was genuinely afraid he might hurt her if he didn't. "That is a *hell* of a thing to think, much less ask," he told her, his voice raw.

"When did you decide?" she repeated. "Maybe you waited until you had a chance to do a little checking—"

"I don't give a damn about the Wildings. I love *you!*"

"You don't even *understand* me, Dylan!" She'd thought, Wednesday night after the ball, that he did. But she'd been wrong. If he understood—much less loved—her, he never would have done what he'd done today.

"Oh, I understand you," Dylan gritted out. "I understand that unless you come to terms with what happened to you when you were growing up, you're going to keep reacting to people and situations the same way you reacted when you were a hurt, confused, rebellious little girl who'd just lost her parents. I understand that you can't keep trying to deny your ten years in Boston without denying a vital part of who and what you are. And I understand that until you find some way to reconcile with your Aunt Amanda, you and I aren't going to have a chance. Because, in some twisted way, you keep mixing me up with her!"

Lily drew a shuddery breath. The force of conviction in what he was saying reached out for her. She fought it away. "There's nothing twisted about it," she said. "You and my aunt are two of a kind. You're exactly the kind of man she—" she gave a humorless laugh, mocking herself more than anything else. "What did she say when you told her you wanted to marry me, Dylan? You did tell her, didn't you? She must have been *thrilled*."

"Lily—" He had told Amanda Wilding of his intentions. He and the older woman had spent several long hours talking that morning. The older woman had made it clear that she knew she'd hurt her niece. Dylan had made it equally clearly that he was not going to allow Lily to be hurt again. "Lily, whatever else your aunt and I may or may not have in common, we both want what's best for you, what's ri—"

"What *you* think is best for me!" she hissed. "What about what *I* think is best? Or doesn't that count with you?"

The question hit him strangely, setting off a disquieting emotional resonance within him. He tried to silence it, but it wouldn't stop. "I—of course, it counts!"

"Oh, really? And I suppose what happened in the Palm Court was a demonstration of how *much* it counts? Dylan, I accepted your *gift*, as you called it, when you took it upon yourself to renovate the playhouse without asking me . . . without saying a word to me. But, if you expect me to accept the 'gift' of your interference in my life—" She shook her head back and forth. "You're so used to doing just about anything you want to just about anybody you want that you think—you think—" She clenched her fists by her sides. "You are not going to renovate me—who I am, what I am, how I live—without my permission!"

Dylan stared at her. "If I'd told you your Aunt Amanda was going to be at the Palm Court today, would you have come?" he asked quietly.

Lily felt as though he was trying to see into the core of her being. Or, maybe, he was trying to see into the core of himself. "No," she answered.

"So, what choice did I have other than to do what I did?"

"You had the choice to stay out of it." From a point of near yelling at the beginning of this confrontation, their voices had fallen to near whispers. But the intensity of feeling remained the same, translated into tone, not volume.

"No, I didn't." Being what he was, loving her the way he did, Dylan knew it would have been impossible for him to simply stand aside. If she truly believed he could have, *she* didn't understand *him*.

Tears pricked suddenly at the corners of Lily's eyes. She blinked them back. "I don't have any choice, either," she told him. She wanted to touch his face one last time, to walk away with the taste of one final kiss on her lips, but she didn't dare risk it. "Good-bye, Dylan."

Dylan let her go. He had to.

Lily stared down at the box office counter, not wanting to make eye contact with any of the chatting, cheerful theatergoers picking up tickets for the opening-night performance of the Potluck Playhouse's world premiere production of *Sleeping Beauty in Space*. In fact, she didn't want to make any kind of contact with anybody, but she had her responsibilities and she intended to discharge them.

"May I help you?" she asked, becoming aware that someone was standing in front of the counter.

"I hope so. Two. In the name of Chase."

Lily's head came up with a jerk. She felt what little color there was in her face—aside from the puffy redness around her eyes—drain away. "Gary?"

Dylan's younger brother stood on the other side of the wire grill that separated Lily from the ticket-buying public. He cocked his head, his easy, open features coalescing into a look of deep concern.

"Garrison Chase, at your service, ma'am," he responded. "And God, Lily, do you look as though you need some service!"

Lily tried to paste a reassuring smile on her lips. It felt crooked and totally unconvincing. She was aware of how devastating she looked. Even caught up in the utter madness of opening-night jitters, every member of the cast and most of the members of the stage crew had noticed her distress and tried to offer some form of comfort. The tiny part of her that wasn't numbed with pain had been touched, but she'd evaded her friends' attentions as quickly as she could.

"What are you doing here, Gary?" she questioned hastily.

"We're going to the play, Miss Bancroft!" a happy young voice informed her. Lily suddenly focused on the fact that Kerri Phillips was standing next to her uncle. The little girl's eyes were shining with excitement. "I was going to come with Uncle Dylan, remember? Only something happened, so Uncle Gary's bringing me instead."

"S-something happened?" Lily faltered. Some of her numbness receded before a surge of alarm. She looked at Gary.

"Dylan's a little under the weather," he told her. "Flu, he says. Me . . . all of a sudden, I'm seriously inclined to think it's heart trouble."

The blood that had retreated out of her cheeks moments before flooded back into them now. "Gary—"

"Uncle Dylan has *heart* trouble?" Kerri picked up anxiously. "Is it bad?"

"Nothing you have to worry about, cupcake," Gary promised, fluffing her long brown hair.

"Well, that's good." The child sighed. "I don't want his heart to attack him or something."

Lily had used the space of this brief exchange to locate the two prime seats she now recalled earmarking for Dylan and Kerri more than a week before. She pushed the pasteboard rectangles at Gary, begging him with her eyes not to ask her any questions.

He did ask one. Fortunately, it was one she could answer without breaking into tears. "How much?" he inquired.

"Oh, they're on the house," she informed him.

"Lily—"

"Really, Gary. I—please. They're comp seats. Third row, center. Enjoy the show."

"Come on, Uncle Gary!" Kerri urged, tugging at his hand suddenly. "It's going to start pretty soon."

"Okay, Kerri." He glanced meaningfully at Lily. "I may not strike you as a knight in shining armor, Lily. I mean, I usually leave that to my older brother. But I'm a good listener."

Lily nodded. "Thank you, Gary."

There was a surge of last-minute buyers after that. Lily was grateful to be kept busy. She didn't want to think too much about what Gary had said . . . or about what he *hadn't* said.

"Hey, Lily!"

Lily finished making change for a twenty-dollar bill, thanked the customer she was helping, then looked over at the source of this salutation. Sam Stevens, clad in jeans, L. L. Bean boots, and a sweatshirt emblazoned with the assertion PORK BELLIES ARE MY FUTURE, ambled over to the counter. His freckled face was unusually serious.

"We're almost sold out," she told him quickly, wanting to forestall the sympathy she suspected might be coming.

"Yeah," he nodded, studying her narrowly. "I think half the dudes from my school are here to catch the laser thing in action. We are talking major anticipation. *Major.*"

"Do you really think it's going to work?" Lily asked. For a second, her mind flashed back to her earlier conversation with Paisley. Lord, how far away it seemed. How much everything had changed in just a few short hours! She'd been so happy. She'd been teasing Paisley, laughing, and, all the while, been looking forward with all her heart to seeing Dylan again . . .

Heart trouble. Oh, yes. Heart trouble.

"No sweat," Sam declared. "It'll be amazing, trust me. Anyways, Mom told me to come out and relieve you."

Lily stiffened. "Why?"

"How should I know? I'm seventeen. Nobody ever tells me why I'm supposed to do stuff."

"Sam—" Lily said sharply. The teenager's gray eyes were shifting back and forth like well-oiled ball bearings, a sure sign he was hiding something.

The shifting stopped. "Maybe she thinks you look

like you could use some relief," he answered bluntly. "I mean, no offense or anything, Lily, but you look worse than the Bride of Frankens—oh, *geez!* What did I say?"

Lily rubbed her knuckles against her eyes and sniffed inelegantly. "Nothing, Sam. It's okay."

"Are you sure?"

"Yes. I'm fine." There was no way she could tell him that it was the mere mention of the word *bride* that had nearly shattered her very fragile self-control.

"Well, look, I still have to take over for you."

She sighed. "It's probably just as well."

"Yeah," he agreed. "I'd tell you to ask Mom for a Valium, but you know that routine she does about needing downers on opening night is a big con. The only thing she pops is Vitamin C."

"I know. Don't worry about me."

"W-e-e-l-l, just a little, okay? See you after the show."

The show was a rousing success. Anthea's remarkable futuristic set drew a gasp of surprise and then a round of applause as soon as the curtain went up. Paisley's clever script clearly won favor with kids of all ages, and the performers made the most of each crowd-pleasing line.

The "laser thing"—which heralded the Slime Monster's entrance and exit as planned, then accidentally went off during the big kissing scene—was an unparalleled triumph. At the end of the performance, the two students who'd designed it were presented on stage and got their own standing ovation.

"We did it! We did it!" Paisley crowed exultantly, throwing her arms about Lily. "Oh, I knew it was going to be a smash!"

Lily accepted and returned the hug, striving to manufacture a passable facsimile of the unadulterated enthusiasm bubbling out of Paisley. "So what happened to the major theatrical fiasco you promised me?" she asked as lightly as she could.

"I'm a director, not a critic. What do I know?" Paisley tossed back, laughing. Then, abruptly, ignoring the swirling madhouse around them, she caught Lily's hand. "Lily, honey—"

Lily shook her head. "If you're going to tell me that *I* look like a major fiasco, don't bother. Sam's already driven that point home with a sledgehammer."

"My son—" Paisley began disgustedly.

"Your son is almost as good a friend to me as you are," Lily interrupted sincerely. "And thank you for sending him out to take over the box office. I just hope I wasn't in the way backstage during the performance."

"Don't be ridiculous," Paisley dismissed the possibility succinctly.

"Yes, ma'am."

Lily spent the next thirty minutes or so circulating. She was in the middle of the predictable postperformance celebration during that time, but she never felt a part of it. It was as though she was enclosed in a plastic bubble: She could see and hear perfectly well, but she couldn't be touched. No one could reach her.

Except Dylan. And she'd said good-bye to him.

Snow White and the Lone Wolf of Wall Street. It had been an improbable, impossible pairing from the very beginning. They'd shared a brief enchantment, and then reality had set in. The fairy tale of love was over.

Lily told herself she was too old to believe in fairy tales. She'd been too old to believe in them for nineteen years.

"Miss Bancroft! Miss Bancroft!" Kerri Phillips's childish treble pierced Lily's melancholy reflections.

The little girl skittered over to her, Gary following in her dancing wake.

"Hello, again, Kerri," Lily greeted her. "Did you like the play?"

"I loved it! It was the best play I ever saw. Wait until I tell Uncle Dylan all about it. He'll be sorry he missed it. Only I'm going to tell him I want to come again. I want to come lots of times!"

"A repeat customer," Gary said with a wry grin. "You can't get much better than that, can you, Lily?"

"No, you can't," she replied.

"And I'm sure that 'Uncle Dylan' is going to be very sorry he didn't come tonight," he went on meaningfully.

"Yes, Uncle Gary, bu-uh-uh—" Kerri broke off to give a tremendous yawn.

"Uh-oh," Gary clucked. "It looks like the Slime Monster must have given you a dose of his sleeping serum!"

"No, sir!" Kerri contradicted with a giggle, then yawned again. "Ah-h-h-anyways, like I said, even if Uncle Dylan did miss tonight, he can come to another show." She looked appealingly up at Lily. "And maybe we can all go out and get something to eat after the play like last time? That was really great. It was so much fun to be with you and Uncle Dylan, Miss Bancroft."

Lily knew she had to give the child some kind of answer. She had enjoyed that "fun" meal after the matinee and she'd enjoyed Kerri's artless company during it. But, more than that, she'd enjoyed the anticipation of what would happen after the meal . . . after Kerri had been dropped at home. She knew that Dylan had savored the waiting as well. Against the backdrop of Kerri's childish chatter, they'd traded glances, brushed fingers, and exchanged bits of food. It had been a dangerous, delicious game for adults only . . . and both of them had finished as winners.

"Miss Bancroft?" Kerri repeated.

"Maybe we'll do it again," Lily told her. A six-year-old child was still young enough to believe in fairy tales.

"Good." Kerri yawned again.

"Okay, time to go," Gary declared. "Good night, Lily. Remember what I said before."

"I will, Gary," Lily answered. "Thank you."

The craziness backstage had calmed down considerably by this time, and the crowd had thinned out as well. Lily knew that the cast and crew—as well as assorted family members, friends, and fans—would be heading somewhere for a party soon. Normally, she would join them. Tonight, she wanted very much to be alone.

No, that wasn't true. Despite everything that had happened, there was still one person—one man—she wanted to be with. But she couldn't be, so she would settle for being by herself, thinking about him.

"Lily?"

The voice that said her name was not one she wanted to hear this night . . . or any night. Or, so she thought. The sound of it made her freeze for a moment, then she turned to face the woman who'd spoken.

"Aunt—Aunt Amanda?"

She *has* changed, Lily thought suddenly. She looks older. More than nine years older. But she looks softer, too. Frailer . . .

"Oh, my dear," Amanda Wilding said. Her voice wasn't quite steady. "I suppose right now you'd probably cast me as the Wicked Witch."

- 9 -

LILY BLINKED. Aunt Amanda seemed uncertain. Almost . . . afraid. Could her aunt, her formidable, unflappable Aunt Amanda, be afraid of *her?* "No, I wouldn't," she said. "I'm too old for that now." She didn't know where the words came from. They simply came, and she knew they were true.

"But there was a time . . ."

"Yes." Lily hesitated, feeling a little as though she was inching her way out onto a very rickety bridge in the dark. If she put one foot wrong, she'd go tumbling to disaster. She took a step. "And there was a time when you probably would have cast *me* as the changeling child—the one you somehow got by mistake."

"Yes," Amanda Wilding admitted.

There was a silence between them then. Something about the silence struck Lily as strange. After a moment, she realized what it was. For the first time she could remember, she and her aunt were sharing a silence, not standing on opposite sides of it.

"Why are you here?" she asked finally.

"Lily . . . I know a great deal about how the past nine years have changed you. I would like you to know how much they've changed me."

Lily had turned away from this woman once today. She couldn't do it again.

"I live upstairs," she said quietly. "Let's go there."

"It's a little messy," Lily said as she swung open the door. "Things get pretty hectic right before an opening, and housekeeping tends to rate very low on my list of things to do." She wasn't apologizing or excusing, she was simply telling the truth.

"I can imagine," her aunt replied quietly as Lily flipped on the lights. She looked around silently for several moments. She didn't seem to be approving or disapproving, just looking. "I see you have another rainbow," she observed.

"*Another* rainbow?" Lily asked, surprised.

Amanda Wilding nodded. "Yes. You had one when you were a little girl, didn't you? When—when your parents were alive."

"That's right," Lily said. "But how did you—?"

"You told me once."

"I did?" Lily brushed her hair back. "I—I don't remember doing that." She gazed at her aunt curiously. She saw a faint, sad smile touch the older woman's lightly rouged lips briefly, then fade away.

"Yes, well, I'm afraid I didn't really hear you when you told me. But I've had time—I remember it now, Lily."

"I see." Lily wasn't at all sure that she did, but she suddenly decided she wanted to. "Sit down, please."

She gestured toward the sectional sofas. "Would you like something? I have tea. Herbal tea. Or wine. And there's some brandy, too. Dylan brou—" Lily broke off abruptly, biting her lip.

"It's all right, my dear," her aunt said after a moment, moving toward the sofas. "I don't want anything, thank you. But if you do, please—"

"No. No. I'm fine."

There was a pause as they sat down. Amanda Wilding's posture was erect and a little ginger. Lily's was more relaxed, but tenser than normal.

We're both uncertain, Lily thought. It used to be just me. But now it's both of us. Oh, yes, Aunt Amanda has changed!

"I . . . was sorry to hear about your divorce," her aunt said after a few seconds, folding her hands neatly on top of her handbag.

"You were?" Taken aback, with her longtime defenses ready to fly up and lock into place, Lily gave the two words a much sharper edge than she'd intended. She was shaken to see a flicker of pain in her aunt's green-gray eyes. Eyes, she realized with a shock of astonishment, that were very, very much like her own.

"Yes, I was." Amanda squared herself slightly. "And not, as you may imagine, simply because of my attitude about divorce," she continued with more than a trace of tartness.

Now *that* sounds like the Aunt Amanda I remember, Lily thought. She was astonished to find she almost smiled at the idea.

The asperity was gone, however, when the older woman went on: "No, the real reason I was sorry when I heard was that I felt—I *still* feel—somehow responsible. If I'd been more accepting of the marriage . . . if I'd been more accepting of Howard—"

"If you'd been more accepting of Howie, I probably

never would have married him," Lily interrupted frankly.

Amanda Wilding went very still, her eyes very searching. "Ah," was all she said.

"So—don't be sorry about the divorce, Aunt Amanda," Lily told her. "I'm not. At least, not now. And Howie certainly isn't. He's married again and he has two children. It may sound a little strange, but I think Howie and I got together for all the wrong reasons, yet somehow managed to break up for all the right ones."

The older woman took a deep breath, then exhaled it slowly. "You're very honest," she said reflectively. "Dylan told me—"

"No." Lily shook her head. "I don't want to talk about Dylan. If that's why you've come—no."

"All right," Amanda agreed, leaning forward. "We won't talk about him now."

"Aunt Amanda—"

"We'll talk about you and me."

Lily stared into a pair of green-gray eyes almost identical to her own for several long, silent moments. Then, slowly, she nodded.

"Good," Amanda nodded in return. "My dear, I made so many mistakes with you . . . and for so many different reasons. A great deal of the trouble, in the beginning, had to do with my feelings about your mother."

"My mother? The family outcast?" Lily didn't try to hide the bitter hurt.

"What the family did was terribly wrong," Amanda said. "I know that. And I shall never forgive myself for being a part of it. But I want you to try to understand—" She knit her fingers together. "You never knew your grandfather. He was a very hard, very autocratic man. He was bitterly disappointed when I wasn't born a son.

I knew it. It wasn't a secret. And I spent most of my time trying to find a way of soothing that disappointment. I . . . I suppose I decided the best way to do that was to become as much like him as I possibly could. As for Jessica, your mother—well, it was entirely different with her. Father delighted in her. She was his favorite. His darling daughter. And she was so very easy to love—"

"And yet you and all the other Wildings rejected her because she dared to love, dared to marry, a man you didn't consider suitable. *My father!*"

"Yes." Amanda didn't deny it. "But Jessica wasn't the only one to love a man the family didn't approve of. I fell in love, very deeply, when I was eighteen. But, unlike your mother, I lacked the courage to follow my heart. I gave him up."

The emptiness in her aunt's voice touched Lily to the heart. Suddenly, things began to get a little clearer. "Aunt Amanda, I never knew—"

"I don't even know if Jessica realized what happened. She was so much younger. And it was all handled very, very discreetly." The older woman's mouth twisted. "I was so angry when your mother ran off. All I could think of was 'why should it be *her* and not *me?*' I was angry at myself, of course. But I directed it at her . . . and your father."

"And eventually at me."

Amanda nodded. "In a way. But not consciously. Please, don't think that of me. By the time you came to live with me in Boston, I'd rationalized, justified . . . I'd convinced myself that I was right and your mother was wrong. So, when you came to me, I made up my mind I was going to mold you into *my* daughter. Not hers."

"Oh, Aunt Amanda!" It was like being given the key to a puzzle. Lily found it a little painful to put all the

pieces together; but once she did, she had a sense of completion she'd never known before. "Oh, Aunt Amanda," she repeated.

Her aunt nodded slowly, her white hair gleaming silver in the loft's overhead lights. "Of course, my dear, you wouldn't be molded to my specifications or anyone else's. When I look back at the things I did to you, the things I said—the way I tried to use the family name, the family money, *anything*—" She spread her hands. "After a time, it became a test of wills. I, in my arrogance, wanted to break yours."

There was a pause. Then Lily said slowly, "I think I wanted to break yours, too." She smiled, just a little.

Amanda Wilding shared her niece's smile. "Lily, I've been very much alone these last nine years. Oh, I've had my pride and my position and all those other things I tried so desperately to make you believe were what truly mattered in life—in people. But, despite that, I've really only had myself to keep me company. And, I can't say that I've particularly enjoyed making my own acquaintance. But, I've learned a great deal. Come to terms with a great many things. And . . . I've kept track of you. You—you've become very dear to me at a distance. You always were dear, but I didn't know it. I am . . . very proud of who you are and of what you are. I'd like to think that I had some small part in it, if only by default."

It was strange, Lily reflected. Only a day ago—no, only an *hour* ago—she would have rejected any claim from Amanda Wilding. She would have rejected the idea that a bond of understanding could exist between them. But now . . .

She saw her aunt make a small movement, as though she wanted to reach out to her. But something stopped her from completing the gesture.

Amanda Wilding had never embraced her niece very often. But Lily could tell, just looking at her, that she desperately wanted to now.

"I think you're responsible for more than a small part," she told her aunt softly. "And it's certainly not by default."

Then Lily Bancroft hugged Amanda Janaway Wilding.

Lily knew Amanda's eyes were damp when the embrace ended. She suspected her own looked suspiciously shiny. She blinked hard as her aunt opened her handbag, took out a lace-trimmed square of linen, and dabbed delicately at the corners of her eyes.

"'A lady always carries a clean handkerchief,'" Lily quoted with a trace of affectionate mischief.

Amanda gave a small laugh. "So, you did listen to some of what I told you," she returned lightly.

"Actually I listened to a lot of it," Lily told her. "But, as far as carrying a clean handkerchief goes—I'm afraid I use Kleenex."

"Yes, well, there's a place for that," her aunt acknowledged, tucking the linen square back into her purse and closing it. She drew herself up slightly, then gave Lily a measured and measuring look. "And now, my dear, I think it's time to talk about Dylan Chase."

Lily stiffened. "No, it's not."

"Why not?"

What could she say? That she had the all-too-familiar feeling that if she gave her aunt an inch on this subject, she'd take a proverbial mile? That her emotions were still far too raw and confused to be picked over by anyone else, no matter how well meaning that other person might be?

"There's nothing to talk about, Aunt Amanda."

"I want to help—"

This time Lily gave the measured and measuring

look. "I know you do," she said. "But . . . what you may see as help, I see as interference."

Amanda accepted this rebuff without reaction. "You love him. That's obvious. And he obviously loves you, given everything he's done—"

"Everything's he's done!" Lily exclaimed. "That's the problem. Dylan is so accustomed to doing things for people, that he just goes ahead and does them. And he's so positive he always knows what's best that he never stops to think of asking a second opinion. Oh, I'm not saying that he doesn't do the right thing. He does. And I'm not saying that he doesn't know best. He usually does. But that's not the point. At least, not as far as I'm concerned. I don't want to have some person always *doing* for me, always *thinking* for me. Not even—no, especially not if that person is someone I love."

"He wants to marry you."

Lily gave a sound that was part desperate laugh, part despairing groan. "So he told me at the top of his lungs in front of the Plaza this afternoon. His exact words were: 'Damn it, Lily! I love you and I want to marry you.'" She shook her head. "You'll notice the wording. He didn't even *ask*."

"Is that why you refused him?"

Lily blinked, telling herself sharply that for someone who'd said she didn't want to talk about Dylan Chase, she was certainly finding a lot to say on the subject.

"Lily?"

She'd gone this far. She might as well finish it. "I didn't refuse him. I accused him of wanting to marry me because he'd found out I was a Wilding."

Her aunt looked shocked. "Do you believe that?"

Lily sighed, feeling very, very weary. "No," she said quietly. "I don't think so. I'm not even sure I believed it when I said it to him. But I am so angry, and the timing seemed so suspicious—and he's exactly the sort of man you'd always said I should marry. Oh, I don't know! It's entirely possible, given the way Dylan acts sometimes, that he decided I was going to marry him weeks ago, only he neglected to tell me because it was supposed to be a surprise."

"I see," Amanda observed softly. "Lily . . . people can change, you know. If you love Dylan—"

"Love may be enough in fairy tales, Aunt Amanda. But this is real life."

"And in real life, people can change."

"Sometimes. If they want to."

"I've changed."

Because it seemed to mean so much to her aunt, Lily acknowledged the truth of what she was saying. And again, because it seemed to mean so much to her aunt, Lily did not point out that the "change" in Amanda Janaway Wilding had been at least two decades in the making.

Roughly forty-eight hours had passed since Dylan Chase had last seen Lily Bancroft, yet the details of their parting were so painfully clear, so achingly vivid, that it might have happened two minutes—not two days—before.

He was sitting in the formal living room of his Fifth Avenue duplex. He'd been avoiding the library and his bedroom. They held too many memories of Lily. The living room was far less evocative. Lily had seemed to have an aversion to it, so they'd spent very little time in there. Dylan hadn't discovered the root of her distaste until he'd brought Amanda Wilding back from LaGuardia Airport Thursday night. She'd commented that the decor reminded her of her home in Boston.

He'd been sitting in the immaculate indigo, ivory, and ebony room for most of the past forty-eight hours, chewing over what had happened and washing it down with Scotch. He'd promised to take Kerri to the premiere of *Sleeping Beauty in Space* Friday night; he'd broken that promise. He'd scheduled a series of meetings with ChaseCo's strategic planners for Saturday; he'd cancelled them without explanation. He'd told his mother he'd attend her monthly champagne Sunday brunch and have yet another talk with Diana; he simply hadn't shown up—he hadn't even called with an excuse.

Dylan closed his eyes suddenly, trying to suppress the image of Lily's face when she'd spotted her aunt and realized what he'd done. But he couldn't blot it out. The hurt he'd seen in her green-gray eyes—the anger, the accusation— would stay with him for a long, long time.

The expression she'd worn just before that—an expression of passionate joy, of loving—would stay with him for a long, long time, too.

Dylan opened his eyes. Someone was pounding on his front door. He suspected it was the same person who'd been ringing his telephone at erratic intervals for the past thirty-six hours . . . the same person who'd been buzzing up from the lobby on and off since the previous night. He suspected it was Gary.

He suspected correctly.

Thud. "Dylan!" *Thud*. *Thud*. "It's me. Gary!" *Thud*. "I know you're—" *Thud*. "—in there. Look, I'm going to huff and puff and call the police if you don't open up!" *Thud*.

After a moment, for reasons he wasn't sure he could articulate, Dylan got up and walked slowly over to the door. After another moment, he opened it.

He had to give his younger brother credit. His stare of astonishment lasted less than a second. Then it was replaced by something jauntily unreadable.

"I figured you'd been stewing in your own juices," Gary said. "But now I see you've been pickling in somebody else's, too." His eyes flicked to the half-empty glass in Dylan's hand.

Dylan knew how he must look. He'd only changed his clothes once in the past forty-eight hours, and that had been about forty-eight hours before. He hadn't shaved since Friday morning.

"If you're asking whether I'm drunk, Gary, the answer is no. Not, I admit, that I haven't been making an effort in that direction," he added flatly. "Why are you here?"

"Would you believe I'm starting a career as an Avon lady?"

"Gary—"

"No, huh? Well, would you believe I'm from the local Welcome Wagon?"

Dylan reached for the door.

Gary shouldered his way in. "Okay, okay," he said quickly. "Much as it sticks in my craw to say this, big brother, I'm here for your own good. And for Lily's."

There was a fractional pause.

"Have you seen her?" Dylan asked, unable to stop himself.

"Friday night at the playhouse. She looked about forty-eight hours less lousy than you do. I also spoke to her yesterday." Gary gave his brother a sharp look. "At least *she* believes in picking up her phone and making polite conversation."

"So, it *was* you calling."

"Yeah," Gary nodded offhandedly. "I was using our secret ring, too."

"Secret ring?" Dylan repeated blankly.

"I thought you were supposed to be the man with the steel-trap memory, Dylan. When you went off to college, you gave me this secret telephone code. Three rings, hang up. One ring, hang up. Then call again. You said you'd always be sure to pick up if you heard the secret ring. I was maybe ten at the time. I felt like James Bond."

Dylan nodded slowly. "I said you should use it if you really needed someone to talk to."

"Right." Gary examined him steadily, his face serious. "Do you want me to go back to my apartment so *you* can use it?"

Dylan gazed back at his younger brother. He did need someone to talk to. "Come on in and sit down," he invited.

It wasn't Dylan's way to open up to others. One of the remarkable things about Lily had been the way he'd found himself able to share so many of his thoughts, so much of himself, with her. He'd spoken to her more frankly about his family and his work than he'd ever spoken to anyone else. She hadn't always approved of what he'd said—and, heaven knew, she'd been quick to tell him so!—but her innate ability to draw him out had been yet another of the qualities that had so deeply attracted him to her.

It was strange to now find himself telling Gary so much about his relationship with Lily. The act of sharing a burden was a very new one to Dylan; and, as with any new act, it felt awkward in its unfamiliarity.

"—so I couldn't ask her," he said. "Knowing what I did. I could imagine how Lily would have reacted if, in one breath, I'd told her it didn't make any difference that I'd just found out she was one of the Boston Wildings, and then, in the next, proposed marriage." He shook his head, raking his fingers through his hair. "Of course, even that would have been better than what I ended up doing."

"Probably," Gary agreed. "On the other hand, what you ended up doing is pretty typical of you, Dylan."

"What?"

"Oh, I don't mean the standing on the steps of the

Plaza yelling. That wasn't at all typical. Which, if you ask my opinion—and I know you haven't—is a pretty hopeful sign. But *telling* Lily you wanted to marry her . . . not asking her: That's typical Dylan Chase."

There was a pause. Then Dylan asked with a slight edge: "Do you think I try to run other people's lives, Gary?"

"Not in the way you mean, no. But—" His younger brother seemed to hesitate.

"But?" Dylan pursued sharply.

"But you don't know your own strength." Gary paused as though trying to put the right words together. "If there's a decision to be made, you make it. If there's a problem to be solved, you solve it. No big deal to you. It comes as naturally as breathing. So naturally, that I don't think it's occurred to you that your strength makes it easy for other people to be weak. It's hard to explain, exactly. But—but just look at our family."

"Our family?" There was a quality about Gary now that Dylan had never seen before. In fact, Dylan felt as though he was seeing a number of things he hadn't seen before. It was as though he was regaining his vision after years of suffering from tunnel vision.

Gary nodded. "Yes. Take mother, for heaven's sake. Oh, she was the original clinging vine, even when father was alive, but you've encouraged her—without meaning to—to cling to the point where it's a miracle she hasn't sprouted leaves. You're always there for her to lean on, so she does. She leans so hard and so often I'm surprised *you* haven't developed a permanent list! And then there's Diana. Well, I kid about her running home to mother whenever she's got a marital problem, or any other kind of problem. But we both know you're the one she really comes crying to. And you've always got a handkerchief ready."

Dylan absorbed all this quietly, watching his younger

brother intently. "And what about you, Gary?"

"Are you asking if I think you've made me weak, big brother?"

"Yes." Was this, then, what was at the heart of the sense of . . . *estrangement* he'd felt for so long? Had what he'd believed were acts of responsibility and supportiveness really been acts that had undermined the brother he'd once been so close to?

"Maybe some people would say so. Some people would probably say I grew up in your shadow, too. But, to tell the truth, I always saw myself as having it made in the shade because you were my older brother. I got into the habit of having you do things, take care of things, for me when I was very young. And I never really got out of it. I suppose it sounds simplistic, but it's like those times when I was a little kid and I used to love to ride around on you, piggyback. You always used to let me hang on as long as I wanted because I didn't weigh enough to cause you any real trouble. It's still a lot like that. I'm still hanging on for the ride. You're still carrying me."

It was like looking through a familiar kaleidoscope tube only to discover the focus had been changed. The pieces Dylan saw were the same ones he'd looked at in the past, but the picture they made was completely new.

No, not completely. It was something he'd been catching glimpses of over the past weeks in Lily Bancroft's company. But rather than recognize it for what it was, he'd dismissed it as the product of Lily's hang-ups and secrets about her past.

"Dylan?" Gary asked quietly. There was a hint of anxiety in his tone, as though he was afraid he might have said too much.

"What you're telling me," Dylan said slowly, feeling an odd smile touch his lips, "is pretty much what Lily's been trying to pound into my skull practically since we first met. Only I couldn't—or wouldn't—listen . . ."

"Oh, I think you picked up a few messages here and there," Gary asserted with a sudden grin. "But—uh—Lily picked herself a tough job. Trying to get through to you. I mean, you've had a long time to develop a—ah—"

"Thick, arrogant skull?" his older brother offered wryly.

Gary's grin widened. "You said it, not me!"

"No, actually, Lily said it."

Oh, my love, Dylan thought suddenly. I've spent so much time trying to "renovate" so many other people's lives that I never saw how much repair my own needed. I do now.

"She did?" Gary asked, brows going up. "She's a gutsy lady, Dylan."

"She's much more than that," Dylan returned, his mind flooding with memories. "You think I'm strong, Gary? Lily knocked me for a loop the second I saw her walk into your office."

"And, judging from what I saw when *I* walked in, you hit her pretty hard, too. Like I said that day, you two are very well matched."

Dylan's voice dropped. "I love her, Gary. I want her in my life. I think I have from the very first. But, beyond that, I need her. The Lone Wolf of Wall Street needs Snow White."

"Then tell her, Dylan," Gary urged.

Dylan rejected this with a shake of his head. He was done with "telling" Lily Bancroft. "I'm going to find a way to *show* her," he declared. "And, once I've done that, I'm going to *ask* her to marry me."

The last thing in the world Lily expected to find when she decided to inventory the prop room was her magic wand. She'd forgotten about its existence.

She'd made the wand four years before for the Potluck Playhouse's version of *Cinderella*. It had been a showy little piece, complete with glitter and gilt. But it had been carelessly relegated to a box of miscellaneous props after the production finished its run. It had stayed there, getting dented and dusty, until she'd opened the carton and found it. Overall, its condition was pretty sad.

But then, Lily wasn't in very good shape, either.

She'd slept very little in the three nights that had followed her good-bye to Dylan. There had been too many thoughts to keep her awake.

Part of what she'd had to think about was the change that had taken place within her. At long, long last, she'd made peace with her past and come to terms with the most important person in it. In doing so, she'd gained a sense of completion.

But, even in the midst of that gain, there had been loss. She'd lost Dylan. That was the main thing she'd had to think about since Friday, and that was the main reason she hadn't been sleeping.

Plopping down on the slightly lumpy mattress of the bed that had been one of the focal points of the playhouse's version of *The Princess and the Pea*, Lily waved her once-shining prop back and forth experimentally. If there were such things as magic, wish-granting wands, she knew what her wishes would be. They would all begin and end with Dylan Chase.

She loved him. It wasn't a fairy tale kind of love. No, it was part of her reality. She knew who Dylan Chase was . . . and what he was. *And she loved him*. It didn't matter that he was, indeed, the kind of man her Aunt Amanda would have selected for her, given the choice. The choice had been Lily's, and she was committed to it heart and soul.

If only she could reach him to tell him so!

Lily stopped gesturing with the wand. Whatever glitter had been clinging to it when she'd picked it up had now fallen off in a flurry of tarnished flakes. "Some magic wand you are," she murmured, and tossed it back into the carton.

She leaned back, bracing herself against the mattress with her elbows. She'd called Dylan's apartment twice on Saturday and three times on Sunday. There had been no answer. She'd even been driven to travel uptown to the building where he lived. The uniformed doorman had been politely pleasant; but he, too, had been unable to get any response.

Lily had called the executive offices of ChaseCo International that morning. She'd been told that Mr. Chase wasn't in and wasn't expected.

She tilted back her head, feeling the heavy curtain of her loose hair move against her neck as she did so. "Oh, Dylan, where are you?" she asked aloud. "I need to see you, to be with—"

She started as she heard a knock at the prop room's door.

"Come back later, I'm busy!" she responded hastily, raising her voice. She'd shut the door because she'd wanted to be alone. Everyone at the playhouse had been hovering around her during the past three days and she'd reached the point where she didn't think she could endure any more sympathy.

Another knock. This one sharp and determined.

"Go away, Paisley!" Lily knew it had to be Paisley. No one else but the redhead would ignore the message the closed door was meant to convey.

Several more knocks. These weren't merely determined; they were downright insistent.

Lily sat up. "Oh, all right! Come in."

Nothing happened.

"I said: *Come in!*" she repeated, staring at the door. What was Paisley waiting for? An engraved invitation?

And still, nothing happened.

Irritated, Lily got off the bed and stalked over to the door. "Honestly, Paisley," she began as she turned the knob and jerked the door open. "I appreciate your concern, but I—*oh!*"

She'd been wrong. It wasn't Paisley Stevens after all.

It was a big frog.

- 10 -

"DYLAN?" LILY GASPED out a split second after she dismissed the possibilities that she was hallucinating or that Gary was playing another crazy joke. She hadn't known she was capable of experiencing so many different emotions, so intensely, in such a short period of time.

She stretched out her hand and touched him, but only once and only for a moment. Her fingertips brushed against his chest as lightly as butterfly wings. She'd had to touch him, to make absolutely certain he was there.

Dylan shuddered a little at the fleeting contact. Not yet, he warned himself. "May I come in, Lily?" he asked softly, his voice slightly muffled by the mask he was wearing.

She nodded. It never occurred to her to refuse.

Dylan stepped into the prop room and drew the door closed behind him.

He was dressed in green sneakers and a green sweatsuit. The color of the sneakers was only mildly obnoxious. The color of the sweatsuit, on the other hand, would have offended even the most ardent vegetarian. Yet, in some insane way, it created a suitably amphibian impression.

The frog face mask he had on was the kind of mass-produced item that children wear at Halloween. It, too, was green and had suitably froglike texturing stamped into it. The eye slits, unfortunately, were uneven, making it very difficult to see out of. The mouth opening, however, at least according to the extremely strange person who had sold Dylan the mask, had been specially enlarged to allow the wearer to catch flies with his or her tongue.

"Dylan, why—?" Lily began, uncertain whether she was asking why he'd come or why he'd dressed up like the Jolly Green Frogman. Any interest in the answer to either of these questions faded as he abruptly shoved the frog mask up onto the top of his head. The sight of his beloved face—a face marked with the subtle signs of stress, yet somehow altered by a new aura of awareness and vulnerability—told her everything she wanted to know. "Oh, Dylan," she whispered, and reached out for him.

He caught her hands and pressed them between his own, enfolding them with warmth and tenderness. When he'd pushed his mask up, he'd breathed in sharply, his nostrils filling once again with the sweet-spice scent of her perfume. He'd wanted to pull her into his arms at that instant, to make himself drunk on the taste of her mouth, the texture and fragrance of her flesh, and the tantalizing movements of yearning he knew her body would begin making against his. But he held back. *Not yet,* he warned himself again.

"Lily," he said, the huskiness in his voice clinging to her name. "I want—I came here to tell you a story."

"A story?" she repeated, puzzled. Couldn't he see she didn't need—didn't want—words? She wanted *him*.

"A story," he repeated. And the look in his amber-brown eyes made her go still, because she realized that he did need words. "Once upon a time, there was a man who believed he was an all-powerful, all-knowing prince. Then one day, after about a dozen years of believing this, he met a woman who made him realize that even if he had been a prince once, he wasn't any longer. He'd become a frog. An arrogant, insensitive frog." Dylan paused, his thumbs moving in unthinking but erotic circles against the backs of her hands. "Oh, he was a frog who occasionally did the right thing for the right reason, but who almost always ended up doing it the wrong way—his way, and his way only. Now, it took a while for this realization to sink in, because the frog had an—" he glanced upward to indicate the mask "—arrogant, insensitive skull. But, once it did, this man knew he didn't want to be a frog any longer. And he knew he didn't want to go back to being—or to at least thinking he was—a prince, either. No, he knew that what he wanted . . . what he wants . . . is to simply be the best man he can be. But that kind of transformation isn't easy. It requires help. Lots of help."

Hope had started Lily's heart pounding as Dylan had begun his story. Happiness made it explode as he finished it. She freed her hands from his and placed her palms gently against his lean cheeks, her eyes going over and over his features. "A kiss is usually what's required," she told him softly.

"One kiss won't be enough."

"No?"

"No. To make a permanent transformation possible . . . there has to be a lifetime commitment to love on both sides."

"If that's the case," Lily said throatily. "Let the transformation begin." And, sliding her hands down to lock around his neck, she went up on tiptoe and offered Dylan her mouth.

One kiss *wasn't* enough. But it was an exquisite beginning. Lips met and melted in a slow, sweet, searing union. Tongues mated in sinuous, supple pleasuring.

One kiss led to another, which led to another, which led to another . . . all strung together by murmured endearments and mounting passion.

Lily felt Dylan's hands move over her shoulders and flow down her back in a liquid, liquifying caress, then claimed the curves of her bottom. He brought her against him, communicating the strength of his desire without words. She rocked the lower part of her body languidly, making a soft sound deep in her throat.

Dylan kissed and nibbled his way from Lily's mouth to her right shoulder. She was wearing one of her oversize sweatshirts again, and it was slipping off on that side. He took nuzzling advantage of the situation. He heard her breathing pattern change, becoming faster and less steady.

"Dylan—" Despite the shivering storm of pleasure he was creating within her with his gently nipping bites and voluptuous licking, Lily wanted more. She wanted it all—everything. She tugged once on his hair.

Dylan finally lifted his head. "I love you, Lily," he said. "I love you."

"And I love you. Oh, Dylan—" She stared up at his face, seeing how his strong angular features were sharpened by passion yet softened by tenderness. His eyes were hazed with topaz smokiness and she knew that soon his eyelids would begin to lower into an expression of deceptive drowsiness.

She was glowing. She had to be.

"Lily?"

"Oh, yes."

For Dylan, "not yet" became *now*. . .

They undressed in haste but loved in leisure. Amid the clutter of props, the trappings of pretended fantasies, they created an enchantment that was utterly right, utterly real. They traveled toward rapture in slow, burning stages. The need for urgency clashed with a knowledge of the inevitable, and time lost its meaning.

For Dylan, Lily was a garden of delights. With word and touch, he planted the seeds of passion. He nurtured her responses, finding them, feeding them, forcing them to flower. Her body blossomed for him as she unfurled her feminine secrets.

He kissed her rosy mouth deeply, gently inscribing the circle of sensitive flesh inside her lips with the tip of his tongue. He visited the tingling sweetness of her peaking breasts with his palms, harvesting their round firmness with a slow, sensual massage that made her womb contract with pleasure. He tested the silken triangle at the junction of her thighs with exploratory fingers, gleaning her hot, honeyed readiness.

Lily shifted restlessly, her blood babbling through her veins like a fiery brook. His hands seemed to be everywhere, his touch tantalizing and tormenting by turns. He would command with one caress, coax with the next.

Her soft brown hair was spread out on the mattress, swathing her flushed face in fine strands of tawny silk. Dylan buried his hands in the glossy spill on either side of her flushed cheeks, restraining the wayward back-forth movements of her head. He brought his mouth down on hers, drinking in her flavor and heat. Lily, suddenly as greedy as he, welcomed the delivering thrust of his tongue.

Anticipation. She quivered as Dylan shifted his weight, moving to straddle her. She opened her eyes, staring into features that were taut with self-control. Lifting her hands, she mapped the hair-roughened breadth of his chest. She teased the knotted buds of his masculine nipples, sipping at the groans of pleasure she evoked as though they had the flavor of vintage champagne.

Excitement. Dylan shifted again, parting her thighs with his knee. His strong hands slipped beneath her, cupping her, cradling her. His breathing was harshly disciplined, but the fires in his compelling eyes were burning out of control.

Ecstasy. He filled her with one deep thrust. She arched up to meet him, wanting them to be irrevocably joined. Mutually possessing. Mutually pleasuring. She lost track of where she ended and Dylan began. But, unlike in the past, she had no fear of being overwhelmed.

Passion was a sea both sweet and stormy. In it, they were each other's anchors. They clung together, drowning in delight.

Aftermath. Tiny murmurs. Slow movements. The small instinctive touches and exchanged glances that are necessary in the wake of the ultimate sharing between man and woman.

"I tried to reach you," Lily said drowsily. "Where were you?"

Dylan smiled. "Heaven. Where were you?" He traced a sinuous design on the upper curve of one of her breasts with a lazy finger.

Lily felt herself flush, as much from the passionate compliment he'd just paid her as from the sensual thrill of his touch. "N-no. I meant I tried to reach you after we—over the weekend. Where were you then?"

His hand stopped. "Hell," he said simply.

Lily knew he was not exaggerating. She had been

there, too. "I'm sorry for what I said Friday."

"What you said was true, Lily. I understand that now. You've held a mirror up in front of my face, my love. I haven't liked everything I've seen in it."

"You are not a frog!" she said with a sudden ripple of laughter at the memory of what he'd looked like standing in the door to the prop room.

"Not anymore," he agreed.

She turned a little, propping her chin on his chest. "Not . . . ever," she informed him fiercely, then melted into gentle laughter again. "Green is not your color, Dylan."

"The clerk at Bloomingdale's who sold me the sweatsuit didn't think so, either."

"What about the person who sold you the mask?" She gave a little sigh of contentment as she felt his hand glide down her spine and settle against the small of her back.

"I don't think you want to know about him. The only place in New York City that stocks frog masks is in Times Square."

"Oh." She tried to imagine Dylan buying the mask. "You—you didn't have to do that, you know. Get dressed up as a frog, I mean."

Dylan sighed slowly. "Are you worried about my dignity?"

"Well—"

"Lily, love. After all I'd done, I had to find a way to show you how I felt. What I'd learned. How I wanted to change. As for my dignity: You once told me you were willing to risk making a fool out of yourself for something you cared about and were committed to. I felt the same about dressing up as a frog. Only I was taking the risk for some*one*."

Lily allowed herself a few moments to bathe in the tenderness of his smile. Then she dropped her eyes, feeling them start to mist with tears and happiness. "You—you were right about my Aunt Amanda," she told him a little huskily. Pursing her lips, she blew gently, watching the movement of his reddish-brown chest hair. "About my needing to be reconciled with her. I don't think that we'll ever be best friends. But . . . she came to see me at the playhouse Friday night and we talked about a lot of things."

He gathered a handful of her hair and tugged at it gently to make her look back up at him. "I'm glad. But, even if everything's worked out for the best, the way I handled the whole situation was every bit as bad as you said it was. And I'm sorry."

She accepted his apology with a smile that told him she'd already forgiven him. Then the smile faded. "Dylan, I didn't mean it when I accused you of only wanting to marry me because I'm a Wilding. That was unfair. And wrong."

Her casual reference to herself as a Wilding assured Dylan that she had made peace with her past. He began stroking his fingers lightly up and down her back. "I do want to marry you, Lily. I was going to propose the night of the charity gala. I've had the ring out of the bank for a week now."

"The ring?" She felt a deliciously feminine thrill.

"It belonged to my great-grandmother. But, don't worry, you've got a choice. If you don't like it, I can have it reset. Or we can pick out something new together."

Lily was certain she'd like it, but she also liked the sound of doing something—anything!—"together." "So, I have a choice of what my engagement ring's going to be like, hmm? What about the engagement itself?" she teased.

Dylan flashed a tempered but nonetheless terrifically sexy version of the killer smile he'd turned on her at their first meeting. "Are you asking whether you have a choice as far as us getting married? What do you think."

She countered his expression with a dazzlingly female look. "I think I've got just as much choice in the matter as you have."

- Epilogue -

"I STILL CAN'T believe we're doing this," Lily Wilding Bancroft Chase remarked to her husband of one year, three hours, and twenty-five minutes. She sipped at the crystal flute of champagne she was holding, letting the vintage sparkling wine dance down her throat.

"Doing what?" Dylan asked lazily. "Celebrating our first anniversary?"

Lily shook her head, her long loose hair rippling with the movement. "No—although it certainly doesn't seem like we've been married a year. What I meant was: I can't believe we're both playing hooky in the middle of a work week."

They were back at Paul and Nora Laurent's bed-and-breakfast in Cape May. Back in the same room they'd had the first time they'd come here. The same room they had every time. They were sitting on the floor in front of the fireplace. A romantically cozy fire burned brightly in the grate. The flickering glow from the flames gilded Lily's soft tumble of hair and burnished Dylan's mahogany thatch.

Dylan grinned. "Well, somebody has to play hooky from ChaseCo now that Gary's stopped playing jokes and joined the firm."

Lily laughed. The complexities she'd detected in Dylan's younger brother had surfaced during the past year. He'd left the Chase Legacy Foundation and gone to work for ChaseCo International as Dylan's executive assistant. He was now on the verge of being sent overseas to take over one of the conglomerate's foreign offices. "Did he really send you a memo about the need for corporate decorum?" she inquired.

"I think he disapproved of the fact that the CEO and the CEO's wife got caught necking in one of the company elevators like a couple of teenagers."

Lily flipped her hair back. "Actually, I thought we were necking *better* than a couple of teenagers," she replied. "He really has changed, hasn't he?"

"We all have."

"Mmm." The smile she directed at her husband was very fond. "At least he took my birthday belly-dance-o-gram in stride," she remarked. In keeping with her threat, she'd found out Gary's birthdate and, with the help of an "exotic message service," had exacted suitable revenge for his stunt with the gorilla.

"True. Several members of the board of directors nearly had coronaries when Fatima of the Seven Veils showed up, but Gary handled it like a pro." Dylan waited a beat, admiring how much of his wife's fair skin was revealed by the pale pink silk dressing gown she was wearing. "I think they're dating, by the way."

Lily's eyes widened and she leaned forward. The loosely wrapped neckline of her robe opened provocatively. "Really? Why didn't you tell me before?"

"Because the first time I saw them together, I didn't recognize Fatima with her clothes on," Dylan replied succinctly.

"Oh."

"But, to go back to the subject of playing hooky. You're not concerned about leaving the playhouse for a few days, are you? I thought you said the latest production is in terrific shape."

"Everything's fine," she affirmed, studying Dylan through lowered lashes. He was wearing nothing but a short burgundy terry-cloth robe. "I probably won't even be missed. With this endowment Aunt Amanda's set up, Paisley's been able to hire three new staffers. There's hardly anything for me to do."

"I'll have to remember that next time you say you can't get away to join me for lunch," Dylan teased her, running a finger up and down her bare forearm.

Lily felt a little quiver of electricity run through her at his touch. "I'd probably join you more often if your idea of lunch wasn't room service at the Plaza."

"I thought you liked room service at the Plaza."

"I do, darling, but you never give me a chance to eat any of the food they bring. In fact, the last two times, you didn't even give me a chance to order."

"That's because room service has a tendency to arrive at the most inconvenient moments."

"You have a point. Oh—incidentally. Aunt Amanda *is* coming down at the end of the month for the Chase Foundation dinner."

"Good." Dylan had become surprisingly fond of Amanda Wilding over the past year, as had Lily. They'd been up to Boston several times to visit, and the older woman generally stayed in one of their guest rooms when she traveled to New York.

"I think she wants to talk to Sam Stevens while she's

down here," Lily remarked, finishing her champagne. "She says she has this wonderful job opportunity for him."

"Oh, no," Dylan contradicted. "Any job opportunities Sam gets are going to be with ChaseCo. I'm not letting someone with his talent slip through my fingers."

Lily laughed. "You may have to fight for him."

"Fine. I'll match any offer your aunt comes up with."

"You may have to match Kerri's offer, too, one of these days," Lily observed with a sparkle. Dylan's sister had gotten divorced from her third husband and moved back to New York City. So far, there was no fourth husband looming on the horizon. Kerri was doing very well, taking ballet lessons and workshops at the Potluck Playhouse.

"Kerri? What's she offering Sam?" Dylan raised his brows as he picked up the bottle of champagne sitting in the silver ice bucket next to him to refill Lily's glass.

"She told him that when she gets a little older, she's going to marry him. Oh, thank you. That's plenty."

Dylan gave the bottle an expert twist to keep the champagne from dribbling out. "I'm going to have to have a little talk with Kerri," he decided.

"Why? Don't you approve of Sam as a future nephew-in-law?" Lily inquired with mock indignation.

"Of course I approve," he retorted. "If he marries into the family, he'll have to work for the family."

"Then what?"

"I want to warn my niece about the dangers of *telling* someone you want to marry them."

"Ah, I see," Lily responded softly. Dylan's gaze suddenly felt very caressing against her skin. She shifted, fiddling with the silk tie belt of her robe.

"And, speaking of marrying . . ."

She slanted him a flirtatious look. "We've already done that, Dylan," she reminded him. She wondered how much provocation it would take to get him to kiss her. Knowing Dylan, virtually none.

"Yes, I recall. What I was leading up to is this."

"This" was a velvet-covered jeweler's box about the size of a deck of playing cards Dylan withdrew from the pocket of his robe. He handed it to Lily.

"What is it?" she asked. The emerald-and-diamond engagement ring on her left hand flashed green and silver lightning as she reached to take the gift.

"Your anniversary present," he said. "Open it, Lily."

After giving him a very special smile, she did as he instructed. She gave a gasp of astonishment when she saw what was inside. She felt the prick of tears at the corners of her eyes. "Oh, Dylan—" she sighed, removing the present from its box. "It's absolutely exquisite!"

Dylan's gift to Lily was a gold locket about the size of a quarter. The locket was in the form of a lily pad, which was sculpted in delicate detail. In the center of the pad sat a small, perfectly made gold frog. The frog had tiny emerald eyes.

"It's so beautiful," Lily breathed, holding the locket in her palm. She looked at Dylan. She knew her heart must be in her eyes.

"There's an inscription," he told her quietly.

She opened the locket very, very gently and scanned the sentiment engraved there. Then she looked back at her husband. "'And they lived happily ever after,'" she quoted. "The end?"

Dylan leaned forward and tugged on the sash of her robe. "No, love. The beginning."

COMING NEXT MONTH

BEST OF STRANGERS #352 by Courtney Ryan
As one comically disastrous encounter follows another, Jenny Shapiro and Tony Coulter agree they've got to stop meeting like this. But catastrophe is beginning to feel normal...and being together as natural as love!

WHISPERS FROM THE PAST #353 by Mary Haskell
Powerfully attracted despite their opposing claims to a spooky old house, Vicki Addison and Mark Rogers sense the mysterious echoes, and inexplicable pull, of a love that may be centuries old...

POCKETFUL OF MIRACLES #354 by Diana Morgan
Burned out and confused, Mallory Taylor hops a ferry to Nantucket and embarks on an adventurous new life—complete with roguishly lovable, forgivably overbearing, irresistibly appealing "Mac" McClintock.

RECKLESS GLANCES, STOLEN CHANCES #355
by Lee Williams
When Claudia Wells inadvertently agrees to a handsome stranger's crazy, tantalizing proposition, she becomes embroiled in a fraud-filled caper and thrilling romantic entanglement of devastating proportions!

BY LOVE BETRAYED #356 by Ada John
Hired under false pretenses, Lainie Wilson acts as companion to the teenage daughter of reclusive, autocratic Paul Reynard—then must divide her loyalties as she confronts the masterfully sexy Frenchman.

LONG ROAD HOME #357 by Jean Fauré
Truck driver Erin Taliferro reluctantly accepts brawny Luke Reardon's offer of help. But his disturbing reticence...and the exquisite tension of their enforced intimacy...drive her into an emotional tailspin!

Be Sure to Read These New Releases!

NO MORE MR. NICE GUY #340 by Jeanne Grant
Thinking his fiancée Carroll finds him tame and predictable, Alan sweeps her away with dashing recklessness and exotic romance—to her secret delight...but ultimate dismay!

A PLACE IN THE SUN #341 by Katherine Granger
Libby Peterson hires casual drifter Rush Mason as groundskeeper for her Cape Cod inn, not anticipating the exquisite tension provoked by his unexplained past...or the undisguised passion in his bold gaze.

A PRINCE AMONG MEN #342 by Sherryl Woods
The joke's on mime Erin Matthews when the devastating man she's spoofing scoops her into his arms, dubs her his princess—and gives her ten days to plan their wedding!

NAUGHTY AND NICE #343 by Jan Mathews
Respectable Cindy Marshall's got scars from when she stripped for a living, and she doesn't need a man to mess things up now—especially not cool, compelling vice squad cop Brad Jordan!

ALL THE RIGHT MOVES #344 by Linda Raye
Coach Ryan McFadden is a *big* man, but five-feet-eleven referee Lauren Nickels is every inch his equal—whether they're battling it out on the basketball court...or volleying sexy innuendos.

BLUE SKIES, GOLDEN DREAMS #345 by Kelly Adams
Joe Dancy appears to be an easygoing farmer with golden good looks and a string of women after him. Yet Sara Scott's convinced he's after something: her money...or her heart?

Order on opposite page